The Dragon & The Dry Goods Princess

Stories By
DAVID ARNASON

TURNSTONE PRESS

Turnstone Press
607-100 Arthur Street
Winnipeg, Manitoba
Canada   R3B 1H3

Turnstone Press gratefully acknowledges the assistance of
the Canada Council and the Manitoba Arts Council.

In recognition of 25 years of support for the arts by the
Manitoba Arts Council and the people of Manitoba, the
author and the publisher are donating a portion of the
proceeds from the sale of this book to the John Hirsch
Memorial Trust Fund which supports the John Hirsch
Award for Most Promising Manitoba Writer.

"Girl and Wolf" and "The Girl of Milk and Blood" from *The Circus
Perfomer's Bar* (Talonbooks, 1984), reprinted by permission.
Some stories were previously published in *Beyond Borders*
and *Hearts Wild* (Turnstone Press), and in *Prairie Fire* magazine.

Design: Manuela Dias

The book was printed and bound in Canada by
Hignell Printing for Turnstone Press.

Second printing: December 1994
Third printing: May 1995

Canadian Cataloguing in Publication Data

Arnason, David, 1940–

The dragon and the dry goods princess

ISBN 0-88801-187-3

I. Title.

PS8551.R765D78 1994   C813'.54   C94-920264-9
PR9199.3.A85D78 1994

for the Willow Island Gang

TABLE OF CONTENTS

THE DRAGON AND THE
DRY GOODS PRINCESS

 nce upon a time, not so very long ago, there was a dragon who lived in a castle in eastern Europe, somewhere near Transylvania, I think. He was happy for the most part, picking off a king's daughter now and again, and spending most of his time sleeping with his head in her lap. Every so often a prince would come by to rescue the king's daughter, and usually he'd just let them go, because after they'd been around too long, they started to complain about the castle and how hard it was to get decent help. So when the prince came, waving his sword and swearing great oaths, the dragon would send the king's daughter out with her suitcase and a purse full of gold. He'd wave good-bye and promise to write, though of course he never did.

But then the communists took over and for a long time it was impossible to find a king's daughter. Just when it looked like things were getting better, democracy arrived, and it's even harder to find a king's daughter in a democracy than in a communist country. Besides, there were a lot of bad feelings with the Bosnians and the Serbs, and one day the dragon's castle was hit by a mortar shell.

"That's it," the dragon said. "I've had it up to here." So he disguised himself as a school teacher, bought an airline ticket, and moved to Canada. He'd always liked remote places, so he found a lake in the Whiteshell area right on the border between Manitoba and Ontario, built himself a castle, and settled down.

For a while everything was perfect. He'd almost forgotten about king's daughters, it had been so long since he'd seen one, and, besides, the fishing was great. Lots of really big northern pike, and perfect rainbow trout in the river just behind the castle.

Then, one day, there was a knock at the castle door. A beautiful young woman with raven tresses stood there. The dragon's heart nearly stopped. He hadn't seen a princess since 1942.

The young woman was talking almost before the door was fully open. "A bunch of us are camped just down the river," she said, "and I saw this place, and I wondered if you had rooms to rent? One night of tenting is all I need, thanks. I mean, I thought canoeing was supposed to be fun, but there's nothing but bugs and slimy fish, and everybody is supposed to do their share. If I wanted to wash dishes I could have stayed at home and done them in a dishwasher. Look. My nails are all chipped."

The dragon surveyed her. Her voice seemed something quite separate from her beauty. "What's your name?"

"Marcia," she answered. "I mean, I've got this big down-filled sleeping bag and an air mattress and everything, but I can't get a night's sleep. First it was a stone under the mattress. Then last night some joker put a pea under the mattress, and I didn't get a wink of sleep."

"You couldn't sleep because there was a pea under your mattress?" the dragon asked, his voice full of hope.

"That's right," Marcia said. "So, do you have rooms?"

"A hundred rooms at least," the dragon told her with some pride. "This is a castle. I haven't even got around to counting them. Tell me, are you a princess?"

The girl gave him a searching look. "What are you," she asked, "a wise guy?"

"No offense," the dragon told her in his most conciliatory voice, "but you looked to me like the daughter of a king."

"That's us," she said. "King's Wholesale Dry Goods, corner of Logan and Main. Hey, what's that crazy outfit you've got on? You into leather and whips?"

"I'm a dragon," the dragon explained. "It's part of the uniform."

"Hey neat," the girl said. "I've never actually met a dragon before. Can you breathe fire?"

"Of course. I'm a dragon."

"Show me. Blast that little spruce tree over there."

The dragon drew himself up and took a deep breath. Then he exhaled slowly and said, "I'm sorry. I can't."

"Sure," the girl said. "You're not a real dragon at all. You're just a creepy guy who lives out in the wilderness and dresses funny."

The dragon was offended, but, on the other hand, he couldn't take a chance on offending a princess. "The forest fire index is a hundred and three point five," he explained. "You're not allowed to have open fires."

"Excuses," the girl said, reaching into her purse and taking out a package of cigarettes.

It was the dragon's perfect opportunity. "Here, let me light your cigarette," he said, and he blew a thin line of flame that ignited the girl's cigarette but also startled her so that she jumped back. "There," he said. "That's proof."

"Hey, terrific." The girl fumbled in her purse and pulled out her package of cigarettes again. "You want a cigarette too?"

"No, I don't smoke."

"What do you mean you don't smoke? If you breathe fire then a little smoke isn't going to bother you."

"Smoking causes cancer," the dragon said with a moralistic tone that he regretted but couldn't help. "Breathing fire does not."

"It just causes forest fires?"

"Only if you aren't careful. Do you want to stay?"

"Maybe," the girl said. "What's the deal?"

3

"You have to let me sleep with my head in your lap every afternoon between three and five," the dragon explained. "You have to bring me cooling drinks before supper on Tuesdays and Thursdays, and I get breakfast in bed on Saturday. You get Sunday off. And in return, you get the run of the castle, an untold fortune in jewellery and gold, and your own telephone and fax."

The girl looked him over critically. "That's the whole deal?"

"Well," the dragon confessed, "there's the usual other stuff."

"What other stuff?"

"Well, you know," the dragon said, shuffling his feet and blushing a little. "The ordinary Dragon-Princess, Beauty-and-the-Beast falling in love stuff. But we can pretty much play it by ear."

"I don't know," Marcia said. "You're kind of cute, but I don't think I'm ready for a relationship."

"Whatever you like. It's just that it's the usual scenario."

And so, Marcia moved in with the dragon, and things worked out pretty well at first. The dragon had been having trouble sleeping without a princess's lap for the past fifty-two years, and so he felt a lot better. Marcia had a lot of fun exploring the castle. There were so many rooms that it was a month before she'd seen them all. She tried on all the jewellery, and counted gold coins until she got sick of counting. The dragon really was handsome, and now that he was getting enough sleep and exercise and eating properly, he cut quite a fine figure. Marcia even fell in love with him, and the Beauty-and-the-Beast thing was more fun than she'd expected.

But by the time summer had gone and fall had passed and they were moving into winter, she started to get restless. The food seemed to be prepared by invisible hands, and the beds made themselves, but she never saw another living soul.

"Look," she told the dragon one day, "it's been thirty below for days. Why don't we slip down to Miami for a couple of weeks? My folks have got a condominium there, it would only cost the airfare."

"I'm sorry," the dragon said, "but I can't leave the castle." He was practicing putting on the castle floor, and it was starting to annoy Marcia.

"Hire a security firm to take care of it," she told him. "There won't be a problem."

"That's not the point," he said, sinking a forty-foot putt. "Dragons have to stay in their castles. They can't just go gallivanting wherever they want."

"Well, I've invited some people out for the weekend," Marcia said. "My folks and my cousin Naomi. I'm going stir-crazy here. We haven't even got cable TV." She hadn't actually invited them, but if the dragon didn't object, then she intended to go ahead.

"You'll have to phone them and tell them not to come," the dragon said. He had expected this for some time. About three months was as long as you could keep a princess happy. Then they got bored and were impossible to live with.

"What do you mean?" Marcia said, now angry. "I told them to come, they're coming. End of argument."

"If they come, I'll have to incinerate them."

"Breathe fire on them?"

"Yes. It's what I do."

"What about the forest fires?"

"It's winter," the dragon said. "The risk is low. Anyway, those are the rules. You're my princess. As long as I've got you, I've got to incinerate anyone who comes near."

Marcia rolled her eyes. "That's ridiculous."

"Sorry. I don't make the rules."

"How am I going to spend all that gold? That was part of the deal. What good is all the gold in the world if I can't spend it?"

"Mail order," the dragon said. "Get the Eddie Bauer catalogue, or Ikea, or something. Anyway, the Dragon-Princess relationship is a two-way street. We've all got to make accommodations."

"So I'm trapped. There's no way out?"

"Not unless a prince comes by and rescues you. The rest is non-negotiable."

"A prince," Marcia said.

"Yes," the dragon replied. "A prince."

Marcia brooded in her room for a couple of days. She didn't know many princes. She sent a lot of faxes, but the few men who even replied said they weren't into rescuing maidens. One of them even sent her a subscription to a feminist magazine. Finally there was only Arnold. Arnold was an accountant who wore thick glasses but he'd been in love with Marcia since grade one. Marcia sent him a fax.

"Who's that guy standing in the driveway holding a sword?" the dragon asked her one morning a few days later.

Marcia glanced out the window. "Must be a prince," she said, "come to rescue me."

"He doesn't look like a prince," the dragon said. "He looks like an accountant. I guess I'll have to go out and incinerate him."

"I thought you didn't incinerate princes?" Marcia said. She'd played down the dragon's ferocity in her fax to Arnold, and she knew she'd feel really bad if he were charred.

"Well, not as a rule," the dragon said, "not a real prince. But if I let a guy like this get away with my princess, I'll be a laughing stock. Next thing it'll be bakers and taxi drivers. I'd never live it down." He walked out the front door onto the porch.

"Hey, you, at the end of the driveway," he shouted.

"Yes?" Arnold answered. He'd taken off his glasses and was cleaning them with the tail of his white shirt.

"Off the property in ten seconds or you're a cinder," the dragon said. He breathed a little burst of fire, not enough to set anything aflame, but enough to convince Arnold that he was serious.

"Just a minute," Arnold told him. "Turn around and look at that castle."

"Yeah. So what?"

"It's falling apart."

"It's supposed to fall apart," the dragon informed him, "it's turning into a ruined castle."

Arnold saw his chance and moved in quickly. In a second he was at the dragon's side. "But it doesn't have to," he said. "That's the beauty of it. Now if you were to put your liquid assets into mutual funds you could repair that in no time and still have enough interest left over for a little holiday. Let me show you." And he pulled a brochure from his pocket and began to annotate figures with his ball-point pen. The dragon didn't have a chance.

And so the princess was rescued. Arnold took her back with him along with bagfuls of gold and jewellery, and the dragon invested in high-risk South-East Asian mutuals and became even richer. Marcia and Arnold took over the dry goods whole-sale business, bought a condominium in Palm Springs, and lived happily ever after.

And as for the dragon, well, Marcia's cousin Naomi came out to visit him, and it turned out that she was a princess too, and so were several other cousins. In the end, there were enough princesses in Winnipeg for a dozen dragons, so the dragon brought over a bunch of friends from Transylvania and they all lived happily ever after, though some of them are still a little nervous when the forest fire index gets too high.

The Coleman Genie

nce, not so very long ago, in the city of Winnipeg, lived a husband and a wife. Nothing about them was out of the ordinary. The husband went to work every day in an office building where he wrote and sent out brochures for the Department of Tourism. His wife worked three afternoons a week as a teacher's aide, and they hoped in the future to start a family and raise a boy and a girl.

One day the husband returned from work and announced that they were going camping. He had been reading his own brochures, and, in his air-conditioned office lit by fluorescent lights, he had caught the camping bug. He had been a little worried that his wife would object. She didn't seem to him the kind of person who liked camping, but, as it turned out, she was delighted. She'd once had a boyfriend who liked camping, and they had tented in nearly every campground in the province. But he'd married somebody else, and every so often she'd see him drive by with a canoe on the top of his car, and she'd be filled with nostalgia.

And so it was, they found themselves in the Spruce Woods

Park on a Friday evening in late June. It was one of those evenings that photographers dream about.

"Wow," Grant said, "this is great. Look at the trees. Look at those sand dunes. I didn't know there was any place like this in Manitoba."

"What do you mean?" Lydia asked him. "You're the guy who writes the brochures. If you don't know about this place, who does?"

"Yeah," Grant said. "Brochures. I just make all that stuff up. But this is the real thing." He swung his arm to indicate the sweep of scenery before him.

"It's too bad we don't have a canoe," Lydia said. "Look at that little lake."

"We can buy one. I'll go out next week and get one."

"Get a seventeen-foot Grumman aluminum," Lydia told him. "They're great." As soon as she had spoken, she regretted it. She had not told Grant about her previous camping life, and didn't want to open up the topic now.

Grant turned to look at her. "How come you're suddenly an expert on canoes?"

Lydia decided that a direct response was best. "I've canoed," she said. "I had a life before I met you, you know."

Grant apologized, as she had intended. "Sorry. Anyway, I'll put up the tent. What was our number?"

"Twelve."

"And while I'm doing the tent, you can unpack all the camping gear."

And so Lydia did. She found an old green stove that ran on naptha. She found a rubber groundsheet, some assorted metal plates and bowls, a few odd knives and forks and a very dirty old green lantern.

In the meanwhile, Grant was ecstatic. He got the tent up, then he went for a swim in the lake. He threw in a fishing line and in no time had two trout, which he fried over the battered old Coleman stove, and they ate them for supper.

Lydia took the dishes over to the cookhouse where there was a sink with running water, and she washed them there. It

10

was beginning to get dark when she got back. Grant was already in the tent, curled up in his sleeping bag.

Lydia opened the flap of the tent. "It's getting dark," she said.

"Yes," Grant agreed. "It's night."

"It's only nine-thirty. I'm not sleepy," she said.

"Look in the camping equipment," he told her. "Maybe there's a flashlight."

"No," Lydia said. "There's no flashlight. I've already looked." But she looked again. "Where did you say you got this stuff?"

"I got it when my uncle George died," Grant answered. He was almost asleep. "He left it to me in his will. I just never picked it up from Aunt Betty until last week. I'm not even sure what's all there, except there's an old Coleman lantern. It must be the first one they ever made. Come to think of it, I don't remember Uncle George ever camping."

"It's pretty dirty," Lydia said. "All covered with dust." Grant didn't answer. He was already asleep.

Lydia examined the lamp. It didn't look like the ones you see in ads, but it was green, and it said Coleman right on it. She began to rub it with a piece of cloth. The lamp seemed to polish very easily. It was soon as bright as new, but Lydia continued to polish it because it was so smooth and beautiful. The lamp began to glow, as if it were lit by neon from within. Then steam or smoke, Lydia wasn't sure which, came out of it, and when it cleared, a small man wearing a frayed tweed jacket and a fedora hat sat on the grass beside her.

"Who are you?" Lydia asked, only a little frightened. The man was quite tiny, and Lydia was sure that she could handle him if the situation demanded.

"My name is Coleman," the man said. "I'm the genie of the lamp. I've been locked up in this lamp in Uncle George's basement for eleven years, but now you've set me free. So you get three wishes."

"You don't look like a genie," Lydia said.

"And you don't look like Cleopatra. Times change."

Lydia thought for a moment. "Can I have anything I want?"

"Anything within reason," the little man said. "But only objects, right? I can't give you health or wisdom or beauty, but pretty much anything plastic."

"How about a million dollars?"

The man looked at her as if he were calculating. "No cash, jewellery, bonds or mutual funds," he said. "How about a little portable gas stove?"

"How about a castle in Spain?" Lydia countered. She was sure she had seen the little man somewhere before, selling second-hand furniture or cars. He certainly was dressed like a salesman.

"I don't do real estate," the man said. "But just a minute ago you and your husband were talking about canoes. How about I give you a canoe?"

"I don't know," Lydia said. "A canoe doesn't seem like the kind of thing a person should use her wishes on."

"It's top of the line," the little man said.

"Fine," Lydia said. "I want a seventeen-foot Grumman aluminum with maple paddles."

"What I can give you," the genie countered, "is a terrific little fifteen-foot Kevlar model. All space-age plastic. It will never leak. You can bounce it off the rocks in the rapids and it just bounces back to its original shape. And a pair of plastic paddles that you can unscrew into two parts for easy transportation. And I'll throw in the life jackets."

"You can't make me a famous actress?"

"No."

"And you can't supply me with an Arab prince?"

"No."

"No Mercedes-Benz, no Ferrari, no Alfred Sung perfume?" Lydia went on. "No Giorgio Armani? Not even Estée Lauder?"

"I'm pretty much product specific," the genie said. "Anything you need for camping. Stoves, outdoor cutlery, coolers, lamps, thermos bottles, waterproof jackets, freeze packs. Pretty much anything you could want."

"Were you always an outdoors backpacking sort of genie," Lydia asked, "or have you fallen from grace? You know, kicked out of the Genie's Union for fraternizing with the customers or something?"

"I beg your pardon?" the genie said. He drew himself up to his full height, which was about four foot two.

"You know," Lydia went on, "this seems pretty demeaning for a genie, shilling for the camping-goods companies."

The genie sat back down beside her. "You've been reading too many kids' books," he said. "That's all nonsense. Princes and castles and all that stuff. I don't get this stuff free you know. I've got a budget. I've got to live with that budget. If I was going to save up enough to give you a castle, I'd have to stay in that lamp for another three thousand years. Look, I used to be in lawn furniture. I've still got some contacts. Give me a couple of days and I could get you a patio set, table, umbrella, four chairs. The works."

"I'll take the canoe," Lydia said.

"You'll take the canoe? Great!" The genie was suddenly full of enthusiasm.

"And a six-man tent with a verandah fly made out of that new nylon stuff that's completely waterproof."

"I don't know," the genie said. "That's pretty expensive."

"You said three wishes. I suppose there's a genie control commission somewhere that I could write to and complain?"

"Three wishes it is," the genie said with resignation. "But try to consider my budget. I've got an old mum in a nursing home. I try to send her a little bit every month. She doesn't have much."

Lydia thought for a moment. "Okay then," she said, "the cutlery set. But the full set, not one of those beginner's sets."

"Right then," the genie said. "I think that's the lot," and he waved his arms. There was a strange noise, something like the air rushing out of an inner tube when it gets a hole in it. And there in front of them was a canoe, a tent, and a cutlery set.

"Wow!" Lydia said. "That's quite a trick."

"You should see a castle appear," the genie said. "Now that's really something."

Lydia's eyes hardened, and she stared coldly at the little man. "I thought you didn't do castles."

"I was just teasing. This is a really boring job, and so sometimes I do that for fun."

"So if I'd insisted on a castle you would have to give it to me?" There was just a hint of anger in Lydia's voice, but the genie didn't seem to notice it.

"Probably. But you've used up your three wishes. *Caveat emptor.* Let the buyer beware."

"Tell me," Lydia said, and her voice was quiet now, "how did you get into the lamp in the first place?"

"Well, I'm not supposed to tell," the genie said, "but since you've been such a good sport, I'll show you. First, I just transform myself into smoke like this," and he suddenly became enormous and bright, as if he were lit from within by neon lights. He was now wearing an enormous turban and carrying a gigantic sword. "And then I crawl inside to look around like this," and he whirled like a tiny tornado and disappeared into the lamp, "when all of a sudden . . ."

The genie never finished his sentence, because Lydia snapped the lid back on the lantern with a sharp click. She could hear a muffled noise from inside the lantern, but she paid no attention to it.

The next morning, Grant woke Lydia up. "What's going on?" he asked her. "Where did all this stuff come from?"

Lydia had her answer ready. "Last night, after you went to sleep, a guy came driving by. Said he was sick of camping. He was all covered with poison ivy. He offered to sell me all this stuff for three hundred dollars. I didn't want to wake you up, so I just wrote him a cheque. Is that okay?"

"It's more than okay," Grant said. "Look at that canoe! This stuff is practically new. You drive a hard bargain."

"Not as hard a bargain as I'm going to drive next time." Lydia said, partly to Grant and partly to the lantern, which she had packed into her own suitcase.

And that's the way it happened. Lydia took the lamp home and let it gather dust for a couple of years. She and Grant tried camping again, but things didn't work out. Grant started to want to take long canoe trips so that he could write his own brochures, and there was a woman in his office who knew a lot about wilderness rapids. Lydia refused to go along, and she brooded about castles. Inevitably, they separated, but Lydia is happy now. Sometimes you see pictures of her in fashion magazines, sitting in a Mercedes-Benz in front of her castle in Switzerland, talking to the Arab prince she recently married.

THE GOOSE GIRL

here was a powerful farmer once, who owned thirteen sections of land just west of Brandon. He had three daughters but no son, and one day he came down with Ludwig's sarcoma. He looked at the lesions on his hands and his feet, and it struck him one day that he would die and that someone must inherit his farm. His daughters were equally beautiful and equally dutiful. They cast their eyes downward when he looked at them, they answered in soft voices when he spoke to them, and they did his bidding without complaint. He decided that he would give his farm to the daughter who loved him most.

When he asked them to tell him how much they loved him, they each answered that they loved him as deeply as their individual hearts would allow. The farmer was dissatisfied with this answer. Ludwig's sarcoma is a painful disease, and his suffering had made him short-tempered. He spoke to them sternly.

"Come," he said, "you must tell me how much you love me or I shall disinherit you all and give my money to the city council to build a new skating arena."

Then the eldest daughter said that she loved him more than a field of wheat that was golden in the fall, and the second daughter said that she loved him more than a field of flax that was blue in the summer, but the youngest daughter said that she loved him as much as she loved salt, for without salt there was no true flavour. The farmer was angered by the youngest daughter's remarks and drove her away from the farm. For a couple of hours she waited with her bag on the highway, until a Grey Goose bus came by and took her away towards the north.

Then the farmer divided the farm between his two older daughters and composed himself for death. To his doctor's amazement, he did not die. A year later, his Ludwig's sarcoma had developed to such an extent that he was in constant pain. By the end of the second year the lesions had covered his entire body, and the doctor published an article about his case in a famous medical journal. By the end of the third year he was mistaken for a leper, and no one would enter his room because of the smell of his sores.

It happened that at that very time a rock-and-roll lead guitarist, temporarily out of work, was hitchhiking across Canada. He had fallen asleep in the back seat of a Jeep Wagoneer driven by a fisherman, who, lonely for company, had picked him up just outside Saskatoon. The fisherman shook him when they had reached the lake where he intended to fish. The lead guitarist asked where they were, and the fisherman told him they were in the Duck Mountains.

"But I wanted to go to Winnipeg," he said. "This is miles out of my way."

"Well, then, you shouldn't have fallen asleep," the fisherman shrugged. "I can't read minds." And he passed him his electric guitar and his hockey bag full of clothes, and left him there.

The lead guitarist was full of dismay. There was no traffic on the dusty unpaved road, so after a while he started to walk. Almost immediately, he met an old woman. She had a large bag and a brown wicker basket.

"Here," said the lead guitarist, whose mother had trained him in gallantry, "let me help you with the bag."

"Thank you," the old woman said, and she passed him the bag. He couldn't believe how heavy it was. "And you may as well take the wicker basket too," she added.

They walked on for a while, and the lead guitarist found the load so heavy that he felt he could go no farther.

"I'm sorry," he told the old woman. "I'm afraid I'm going to have to stop for a rest."

"Oh, no you don't," said the old woman, and she jumped up on his back. The lead guitarist found that, tired though he was, he could not stop walking, and he could not put down his load. He was sure his heart would stop, but it didn't, and at last they turned off the road and made their way to a farm house. The geese came cackling to meet them, bending their necks and raising their wings and hissing. Behind them came another woman, tall and well-made, but so ugly and wrinkled that the lead guitarist could hardly bear to look at her.

"Are you all right, Mother?" the girl asked.

"Perfectly fine," the mother replied. "This young gentleman has just been kind enough to give me a lift home." And with that she sprang from his back as spry as could be and picked up the bag and the wicker basket as if they weighed nothing. "Come," she said to the lead guitarist, "you've been a perfect gentleman, and you should be rewarded. But first," and she indicated her daughter, "you had better go in the house and wait. I can't let you stay alone with this young man. He might fall in love with you."

The lead guitarist thought to himself that even if she were twenty years younger he would not fall in love with a woman so ugly, but he decided not to offend the old woman by saying anything. The old woman went into the house with her daughter, and, because it was a languid afternoon and the gentle breezes from the south soothed and comforted him, the lead guitarist found a soft spot in the grass and fell asleep.

When he woke up it was early morning and the old woman was feeding her geese. They cackled and hissed and seemed to love her a great deal. The lead guitarist was embarrassed when he realized that he had slept the whole night away without even awakening, but the old woman laughed and said, "The young need their sleep. Now it's time for you to be off before my beautiful daughter comes out to care for the geese. Take this." And she handed him an emerald box with a tiny gold catch. "It will bring you luck." The lead guitarist shoved the box into his pocket and hurried off without even looking back. He did not want to take a chance on seeing the beautiful daughter with her wrinkled skin.

For three days he wandered in the wilderness with neither food nor drink, until at last he hitched a ride with an Old Dutch potato-chip delivery truck. The driver let him off at a beautiful farmhouse just west of Brandon. A farmer and his wife were sitting in lawn chairs on the porch, and the lead guitarist, who by this time was weary and hungry, decided to ask them for food. As he approached them, it became clear that the farmer was in pain. He was covered with sores and he smelled very bad. The lead guitarist recognized the signs of advanced Ludwig's sarcoma, but he approached the couple anyway.

"Oh, if only I could die, what a happy man I would be," the farmer moaned.

"Everything would be all right if you hadn't driven our youngest daughter away," the wife replied.

"What could she have done?" the farmer moaned. "My two eldest daughters run the farm even better than I could have done myself. They love me and bring me gifts. All my youngest daughter ever gave me was ingratitude."

The lead guitarist realized that he had come at an unfortunate time. Nevertheless, he decided that he would try to speak with them. He reached his hand into his pocket and discovered something smooth. He pulled it out and realized that it was the emerald box the old goose woman had given him. On an impulse, he gave it to the farmer's wife, saying, "I'm tired and hungry, and I would like food and rest. In return, let me give you this fine emerald box."

The farmer's wife took the box, but as soon as she opened it, she burst into tears. Inside was an oval portrait of a beautiful young woman. The lead guitarist looked at the portrait. At first glance he thought it was a portrait of the goose woman's daughter, but on closer examination he discovered that the girl in the portrait was smooth-featured and beautiful. The farmer himself refused to look at the portrait.

"Where did you get this portrait?" the farmer's wife asked.

"It was given to me by an old goose woman," the lead guitarist answered. "She lives north of here in the Duck Mountains."

"We must go immediately," the farmer's wife said. "This woman may have information about our missing daughter." The farmer grumbled, but he went out to the garage to get the 1987 Buick Electra that he loved nearly as much as he loved his daughters. While he was getting the car, his wife made a roast beef sandwich for the lead guitarist and served him a light beer with it. After that, the lead guitarist felt much better, and they headed north to the Duck Mountains on Highway 10. The Buick was very comfortable, and even in the back seat there was plenty of room for the lead guitarist's long legs. The farmer's sores gave off an unpleasant smell, but with the window rolled down a couple of inches, it was bearable.

In less than three hours, they were in the Duck Mountains, but, try as he might, the lead guitarist could not find the old goose woman's farm. Finally, he recognized the spot where the fisherman had left him and where he had first met the old woman.

"Leave me here," he requested. "I will walk along the road until I find the place. I shall make all the necessary inquiries, and if you meet me at this spot tomorrow, I will have information for you."

"But what are we to do for the whole evening?" the farmer grumbled. "We can't just drive around the countryside."

"There is a wonderful motel in Swan River," his wife informed him. "It has a heated swimming pool and a cocktail lounge famous for its Bloody Caesars. We will stay there." The farmer continued to grumble, but drove down the slight slope of the road and disappeared around a curve.

The lead guitarist started down the road himself, though it felt both strange and familiar. He was sure it was the same road he had walked before. He recognized details, a bent oak tree, a spruce that had been struck by lightning, but nothing was the same. Everything seemed outlined quite separately and distinctly. After a few moments, he realized that it was dusk. Shapes began to lose their outlines. In the southeast, a full moon changed from yellow to silver.

Then the lead guitarist heard a noise behind him, the cackle and hissing of geese. He looked back and saw that someone was coming down the road, driving a flock of geese before her. The lead guitarist slipped off the road and down a small path that led to a lake. He thought he would wait there until the geese and their driver had passed, but suddenly the noise grew louder, and he realized that they were coming to the lake. The first geese were already into the clearing when the lead guitarist clambered up the rough trunk of a tree and hid himself in its lower branches.

He was barely hidden when the young woman and her geese arrived. He recognized the goose woman's daughter as she drove the geese to the lake. He sat in the tree, scarcely daring to breathe as she took off all her clothes. He hardly dared look at her wrinkled body, but then, she took off her skin and shook free her long blonde hair. Before him was the most beautiful girl he had ever seen. Her skin was as white and smooth as ivory. And there was no doubt that she was the farmer's beautiful daughter. She looked exactly like the oval portrait, but that portrait had shown only her head and shoulders, and here there was much more to see. She began to sing in a sweet melodious voice, and the lead guitarist realized that he had never heard anything more beautiful. It struck him that a rock band with a lead singer like her would be famous in no time flat.

The lead guitarist had been concentrating so hard on the beautiful girl that he forgot where he was sitting, and before he knew it, he had tumbled out of the tree with a noisy crash. In a second the girl was gone, back down the path, and the geese rose from the water as one, cackling and hissing, and they too disappeared. All that was left was the wrinkled skin, and when the lead guitarist picked it up, it crumbled into dust.

All that night the lead guitarist wandered, but he was unable to find the old goose woman's farm. The next morning, tired and sore, he made his way to the spot in the road where he had agreed to meet the farmer and the farmer's wife. They were waiting for him when he arrived, and they greeted him with excitement.

The lead guitarist told them his story, and, though they were happy that their daughter was alive, they were distraught that she could not be found.

At that very moment, they heard the cackling and hissing of geese, and from the woods emerged a flock of snow-white geese, followed by the old goose woman and the beautiful youngest daughter of the farmer and his wife. The farmer's wife was filled with joy. She hugged her daughter and asked, "Have you been kept captive by this horrible old woman?"

"No," the daughter replied. "The goose woman is the kindest person in the world. For three years she has protected me from harm. I owe her my deepest thanks. And now," she said, turning to her father, who had become quite pale, "it is time for us to make up." And the third daughter, the youngest and the most beautiful, who is always death, took her father in her arms, and paying no attention to the sores on his cheek, she kissed him.

"Thank you," the father said, and he died there in her arms.

"You have released him," the farmer's wife said. "Since you left he has yearned for death, but he has not been able to die. Unfortunately, I will not be able to reward you because your father gave everything away to your two sisters."

"It doesn't matter," the third daughter said. She went over to the lead guitarist and put her arms around him. "I will sing with this handsome prince in his rock band, and I will play the tambourine, and we will be wealthy beyond the dreams of avarice."

And it came to pass exactly as the girl had predicted. Within a month they were signed to a long-term record contract, and within a year they had a North American tour. Within five years, they had three daughters, and the youngest was the fairest of them all. The lead guitarist loved all three. The eldest was gentle and giving, and the second was lively and loving. But he loved the youngest and fairest the best, even though every time he took her in his arms his heart slowed and went cold.

THE COWBOY: A TALE OF THE OLD WEST

ut on the prairie, alone on his horse, the cowboy yearns. In all that dust, the hot mid-day suns of summer, he yearns. He yearns through the rain that drips from his Stetson, yearns through the bitter cold and snowy days of December, yearns through the awful western springs when horseshit starts to peek out from the snow like some obscene early flower.

He yearns for the rancher's daughter, that goes without saying. Susan, the rancher's blonde and blue-eyed daughter, who can rope a calf, geld a steer, ride in the rodeo with the toughest of men. Susan in her soft tan cowboy boots. He imagines her wearing only her boots, naked, swinging in her hand the lariat, the lasso. He imagines the burn of the rope on his skin.

He yearns for the lady teacher, Miz Hawkins, her soft black curls and her big brown eyes. She stands for goodness and wisdom, and he loves her voice. He imagines her naked, wearing only her eastern high-heeled shoes, carrying a book. She tells him over and over, no, that is wrong, you must do it again and again until you get it right.

He yearns in the arroyos, yearns on the burning prairie, yearns on the mountainsides. When he walks along the barbed-wire fence, putting in a new staple here, steadying a post there, he yearns for the bright-lit taverns of the town, yearns for the smooth rye whiskey and Seven Up, the polished oak of the bar. He dreams then of Miz Sally and her girls, those high-stepping dancers, flashing flesh under their lacy crinolines.

Around the fire with the other cowboys he makes rude jokes about the rancher's daughter, about the schoolmarm from the East, about Miz Sally and her girls. He eats his bacon and beans, wiping up the juices with fresh bread the cook has just made today, and he leans back on his bedroll and yearns.

When he sleeps, he dreams of houses, ranch houses made from logs, with pine floors and curtains on the windows. He dreams of white stucco houses with brightly coloured furniture, solid brick houses with horsehair chesterfields, glass houses on golden beaches where the waves pound in every day. Sometimes he puts his women in these houses, Susan, the blue-eyed rancher's daughter, Miz Hawkins, the eastern schoolmarm in her high-heeled shoes, Miz Sally and her girls, dancing. When he does, the dreams come apart. Cattle get in them, lowing herds of steers, and cards, diamonds and clubs, the ace of spades. The next morning, his yearning is unfocussed, the weather is bad.

The cowboy's heart is filled with love. It overflows. He has no place to keep so much love, and so he scatters it around him recklessly. He bandages the injured foot of a calf with enough tenderness for an entire orphanage. He finds butterflies made sodden by the rain and carries them to rocks in the sun where they can dry their wings. He comes on a coyote with four kits, and he doesn't kill them, though he has been instructed to do so. It is part of his job. He has so much love that he doesn't even pick up the little ones to cuddle them. He just watches them playing in the light, and he rides on.

He rides on. This is how his days pass. He rubs the flank of his horse, touches the worn leather of his saddle, the worn wooden stock of his gun. He keeps his eyes focussed in the distance because of the unbearable beauty of the prairie. He must get the herd to market. He cannot stop for fringed gentian beside a rock, spotted touch-me-not on the edge of a swamp, Indian paint brush and wild columbine on the higher slopes. Sometimes he imagines the bouquets he might take to Susan, the rancher's blue-eyed daughter, masses of orange wood lily and purple iris. Miz Hawkins, the eastern schoolteacher, will get a single wakerobin, picked before the snow has gone. Black-eyed Susan for Miz Sally, and asters for her girls, depending on the season: white asters in June, yellow in August and blue in September.

And when the rustlers have come by and stolen some of the herd, he yearns for the good old days when he might have followed their trail into the mountains, confronted them, dark-haired slouching men in black hats, and brought them to justice. Then he might have won the heart of the rancher's daughter, he might have shown his sense of justice to the teacher, he might have won the admirations of Miz Sally and her girls.

Now there are only the tracks of the refrigerated trucks that the rustlers drive, a few hooves and horns on the bloodstained grass. The rustlers have even taken the skins to tan. There are not enough entrails left to feed the coyotes for a single night. And when the sheriff comes, the cowboy must fill out forms in triplicate, and have them stamped.

Tumbleweeds drift across the plains. Dust devils whirl and throw dust up into the cowboy's eyes. There is always a thaw in February, a false spring when icicles drip from the eaves of the bunkhouse and the sparrows gather in flocks and twitter their praise. Then the cowboy is filled with desire. Desire gets into his joints, and it makes it hard for him to walk. Desire fills his stomach, so that he cannot eat, and he loses weight. Desire rages in his brain like a fever, like a furnace. He tosses in his bunk and his eyes refuse to see, they keep out the light. Finally, the doctor comes and cures his desire with antibiotics. The cowboy wakes up to see that the rancher's daughter is wiping his brow with a damp cloth, but his desire is gone now, and what he feels for her is gratitude.

The cowboy thinks there must be something wrong with him. He is a creature of excess. He is too tall. His feet are too large. He laughs too loudly. He knows too much about the art of being a cowboy, knows when the herd is restless, where the lost calf has gone, where the wolves are stalking, where there might be bears. He can guess the weight of a steer to a pound. He can break the toughest horse, he can carry a heavier load than any of the other cowboys and be the least exhausted at the end of the day. The problem, he thinks, is that there is too much inside him. There is no room for anything more. And there is no place where he can put the excess he carries with him. He thinks that he needs a wife. And he needs children. That will do the trick, he says to himself. That will do the trick.

The cowboy yearns for his unborn children, the strong-boned boys, the lithe daughters who will spring from his loins. He basks in their future respect, their filial admiration. He imagines the family photo, the four boys and three girls arranged around a cowboy and his wife. Perhaps they will use it on their Christmas card.

Alone on the prairie under a starry sky, the cowboy fears his death, not as an abstraction, but as a real event. His fear is on the edge of panic. He becomes hot and flushed. He feels death on his joints, death as an icy hand gripping his heart, death as a ball of cancer growing in his heavy body. He cannot catch his breath. The horizon is on fire.

Sometimes the cowboy hears wolves in the distance. Sometimes he hears laughter. On summer nights when he is camped near the town he can hear the music from the Saturday-night dance. Then he thinks of the bare arms of women, their calico dresses and their perfume. He yearns to dance, to form a square, to dosey-do, to allemande left, to over-and-under. He wants to give his body to the violins and the accordions.

The cowboy wants to submit to something. He wants to be taken by something larger than he is. He wants to give up all responsibility for himself and hand his life over to someone else so that he needs only to follow orders. But this is impossible.

He is a cowboy. One moment of inattention and the herd will be lost.

The cowboy is building up his grubstake. Every payday he sends some money to his mother, he has a night on the town, and he puts a few dollars into a leather wallet he keeps in his bedroll. When he has enough money, he will start his own spread. Then he will no longer be a cowboy, but a rancher himself.

The cowboy rides into sunsets and into sunrises. He rides into the blackness of night and into the brilliance of noon, but something is wrong. When the ride is over, he is still there. Nothing has changed, and no one is watching. The great herd lows softly. Smoke lingers in the air.

When the yearning is too great, the cowboy takes his rifle to the dump. He fires at empty bottles, watching them explode. He fires at the furtive rats, watching them explode beside the broken glass. He shoots out the insulators of the telegraph wires, and the next day there are no messages in the town. The dry grass crackles under his feet.

When he finally acts, it is almost too late. When he asks if he may speak to Susan, the rancher's blue-eyed daughter, he is told that she has gone to law school in the East. The rancher shows him a photograph. The cowboy knows that the woman in the photograph is never coming back. He remembers her cool hands on his forehead the time he was cured of desire. Her soft tan boots are still in the closet.

When he goes to town, the wedding has already begun. Miz Hawkins in a white dress and red high-heeled shoes is marrying the banker. The whole of Main Street has been closed off, and there are free barbecued steaks for everyone, free rye and Seven Up at every corner. The cowboy joins hands with everyone else and sings "Auld Lang Syne," before the banker and his wife leave for a honeymoon in the East.

In the tavern he meets Miz Sally and buys her a drink. She is returning to Boston to open a millinery shop. She has made her grubstake in the West, and now she is returning home. Her girls have no place to go. The cowboy looks the girls over and chooses Dorothy, who is neither plain nor pretty, and he marries her that day in front of the justice of the peace.

He buys a ranch and raises sons and daughters. He is saving money to send his daughters to law school in the East. His boys will all be bankers, and they will marry schoolteachers. His house is glass and stucco, and it looks over the river. From where he stands, he cannot see the prairie beyond.

The horizon is on fire. The smell of smoke is everywhere. The grass crackles underfoot. Coyotes howl in the distant hills. Gophers and foxes and deer plunge into the river. The air is filled with whirling birds. The cattle are maddened by the flames and the smoke, and they bellow in rage and fear, but there is no cowboy to save them. The rancher, in his glass and stucco house, is facing east.

THE STAR DOLLARS

here was a girl once, born on the windswept
prairie a few miles south of Boissevain, whose
father and mother had died, in the way of fathers
and mothers, the father, drunk one night
crashing his Skidoo into a municipal snow-
plough, the mother, slowly disembowelled by a doctor who
gave her a hysterectomy, removed a kidney, took out her
gallbladder, removed her appendix, until finally he had
hollowed her out completely.

And the crops failed as they do on the windswept prairie
and the locusts came and hail and tornadoes and long cold
winters followed by drought and sun scorched summers so
that the trees died and the grass turned brown and the soil
was blown from the fields. And in the end the banker came,
and the lawyers and the auctioneer and the friends and the
relatives until at last there was nothing left, not a hoe nor a
rake nor a shovel, not the doilies her mother had made nor
the silver spoons from Niagara Falls and Hamilton, not her
father's collection of pipes nor his Ithica Featherlight
shotgun, not her own Barbie doll nor the blue ribbon her calf

had won at the winter fair in Brandon.

And so she had neither room to live in nor bed to sleep in, neither roof nor floor, and she had only the clothes she wore and a slice of bread the waitress at the cafe at the Esso service station had given her. And when she was forsaken, when she was bereft of all hope, when no one could help her any more because they all had their own lives to lead, she walked out into the fields of wheat and barley, into the fields of flax and canola and rye.

And of course she met a poor man, she had always known she would, and when he cried for food she gave him the entire slice of bread, because she was good and generous, because when you are asked for a slice of bread it is hard to refuse even if you are hungry yourself.

And she met a child, as she knew she would, the child cold and weeping, and she gave the child her bonnet to keep it warm. And the next child was also cold, all the children were cold, and she gave it her bodice, to keep it warm even as the third child claimed her blouse, and she had only a shift to keep the wind from her own body.

And she came to a forest. Outside the town there is only field and forest, and if you walk through the field you must come to the forest, and she found a child there, at the entrance to the forest, a child weeping for the cold. She gave her shift to the child, and she walked naked into the forest saying to herself, "It is dark in the forest. No one can see me here."

And she walked in the forest, naked in the darkness, and she knew that now she had nothing left, she had lost everything that she had ever had in the world. And as she walked, she realized that, though she had nothing else, she had her nakedness. And as she ran her hands across her body, she realized that it was not a shameful nakedness.

The stars above the forest poured down their light on her, and she prayed that they would shower her with dollars. But though she stood there a long time, they gave her nothing but their cold light. And after a while she became bolder in her nakedness, and in the morning she met a woodcutter who loved her for the bravery of her nakedness and he took her home and bought her a fancy dress and gave her food. But she refused the dress and took her confident nakedness to town, where the mayor offered to marry her and the banker offered to give her back the farm. But she refused them both and took her brilliant nakedness to the city, where she was toasted and cheered and offered great wealth. But she said no and she took her blinding nakedness to the capital, where princes vied for her hand, and she became a great star in the movies, and the dollars poured down from heaven onto her there where she stood.

THE HOAG BROTHERS & THEIR ADVENTURES IN REAL ESTATE

nce upon a time there were three brothers, James, Robert and Bruce Hoag. They owned a factory that made futons and pine furniture that looked vaguely Swedish, and so they did quite well. They all lived together in the Ashdown Building, a remodelled warehouse right downtown, so that they only had to walk across the street to get to any of a half-dozen singles bars. But they weren't happy.

One day James, the youngest of the Hoag brothers, had had enough. "Look you guys," he said, "I've had it up to here. There is no privacy at all in this place. I spent forty dollars on gin just to get that blonde from Harvey's Bar to come up here, then I find you guys playing rummy on the dining-room table. You are ruining my sex life."

"You don't have a sex life, James," his brother Bruce told him, without sympathy. "You might have if you lost forty pounds, but you're lucky we were here. If she'd seen you without your girdle she'd have died laughing."

"Oh, sure, Bruce," James replied. "The pot calls the kettle black. Anyway I've had enough of it. This is not going to

35

happen again."

"Yeah?" Robert said. "What are you going to do about it?" He was the middle brother and so he could be sympathetic both ways.

"I'm going to build myself a house."

"You're crazy," Bruce told him. "Have you looked at the cost of houses lately?"

"Well, maybe not a house then," James conceded. "I'll settle for a cottage. I'll get a package from a lumberyard and build it myself. And you guys are welcome to visit. But if I come home with a chick, it's out you go."

And so James, the youngest of the Hoag brothers, decided that he would build himself a cottage out at Grand Beach. He found a lot with a nice view of the lake, and he put in an offer with a real estate agent. Then he went to Canadian Lumber to get prices on cottage packages.

When the clerk told him the price of the package he had been considering in the catalogue, he could hardly believe his ears.

"Thirty thousand dollars?" he said. "Are you insane? I want a cottage, not the Taj Mahal."

"Well, the Cedar Package would come in at about twenty," the clerk said. "That's unassembled of course."

"Twenty thousand?" James still found the figures outrageous. "These are the Cedars of Lebanon?"

The clerk was losing patience. He didn't earn enough money to even consider owning a cottage himself, and James's expensive suit offended him. Still, he checked his temper. "How much were you planning to pay?"

"I was thinking four, maybe five grand. And that's including the deck."

"I've got a package here," the clerk said. "Forty-five hundred, deck included. Straw. Only you've got to assemble it, and you have to find your own clay."

"Straw?" James couldn't believe the clerk was serious. "Straw is a building material?"

"Oldest building material in the world. Cool in summer, warm in winter, makes a great roof."

"I don't know," James said, but in the end he was convinced. New techniques developed in Finland, the clerk told him, made building with straw an entirely different proposition.

And so it was that the youngest of the Hoag brothers built himself a cottage of straw. It was really a very pleasant place, not quite on the lake, the lakefront lots were a bit too expensive and they'd turned down his first offer, but only a fifteen-minute walk down to the water. He started playing beach volleyball, and in no time at all he had a Swedish girlfriend named Bibi and she spent quite a bit of time with him at the cottage.

The other brothers didn't get to meet Bibi, but they heard a lot about her, her soft blond hair and her shining teeth. And so they too were set to thinking. Robert, the second brother, didn't see why he shouldn't also have a cottage, and incidentally a girlfriend. And he too went to Canadian Lumber.

"Ah yes, Mr. Hoag," the clerk said. "We sold a package to your brother, and he seems to be perfectly satisfied. I suppose you would also like a fiscally conservative package?"

"What do you mean 'fiscally conservative'?" Robert asked.

"Well, actually, it's the economy package."

"The economy package?"

"Straw. A straw house."

Robert pondered for a moment. "I was thinking sticks," he said. "Boards in fact. The Cedar Package."

"Ah, well, I have just the thing," the clerk said, and he pointed out the Voyageur model in the catalogue.

And the same thing happened to Robert. He bought a cottage in Victoria Beach, not actually on the beach, but in sight of the lake. And he joined the Victoria Beach bridge club, and in no time he too had a girlfriend, who coincidentally, was also named Bibi. And he also bragged to his brothers, but made sure that they didn't come by and cramp his style.

The third Hoag brother, Bruce, the oldest of the three, began to get lonely. He was the most conservative of the brothers, but also the most fully aware that life was passing him by, and so he too visited Canadian Lumber.

"Brick, you say?" the clerk was incredulous. "Not many people build cottages of brick."

"Brick is what I said," Bruce told him without hesitation. "I want a cottage that will last. And there's been a lot of break-ins lately. I want security."

"And where is this to be delivered?"

"Winnipeg Beach. Right on the lakefront. Oh, and I'll want a skylight."

"Skylights are extra," the clerk said. He worked on commission and he wanted to sell as many options as he could without actually scaring the customer away.

"Fine," Bruce said. "A skylight. Oh, and a hot tub. The biggest hot tub you've got."

"Yes, sir!" the clerk replied, and it was all he could do not to click his heels together.

And the third brother moved into his cottage and joined the Winnipeg Beach golf club. He didn't meet many women, but he met a lot of retired bankers, and before long they were investing in the business, and Hoag Brothers Furniture was doing very well indeed. He hardly ever saw his brothers these days.

Meanwhile brother James ran into a little problem. He asked Bibi to marry him, and she agreed, providing he would transfer the cottage into her name. She'd been very poor in Sweden, and she needed some individual security so that she could feel herself an equal in the relationship. He agreed of course, and had a deed drawn up, Primrose Cottage, Grand Beach, Bibi Wolff, Proprietor.

And then one night, only a few weeks later, there was a knock at the door. There had been several break-ins lately, so James was a little worried. He opened the door to the limit of the safety chain and peered out. It was Bibi.

"Come on in," he told her, and he opened the door. She looked even more beautiful than usual, framed in the light.

"I'm sorry James," she said, "but I'm afraid it's over. I'm in love with another man."

James was beside himself with grief and rage. "Another man?" he bellowed. "Who is it? I'll murder him."

38

"I'm afraid that's none of your business" Bibi told him. "Oh, and by the way, you'll have to move out. I want you out of here by the weekend. I'm having some friends down."

"But it's my cottage!"

"Not any more. See this deed?" And she took out the paper that James had signed just the other day. "It says Bibi Wolff, Proprietor."

And of course she was right, and so poor James was sent out into the cruel world. He went down to Victoria Beach to visit his brother Robert, hoping for sympathy.

When Robert answered the door, he found a heartbroken James.

"She left me, Bob," James said. "She took me for everything I had, and now she's gone."

Robert was full of sympathy. He poured James a glass of scotch and consoled him as best he could. "That's terrible," he told James. "And just when I had some good news to tell you." He walked over to the window and looked out thoughtfully. "James," he said. "I'm going to marry my Bibi!"

James didn't seem to notice what Robert had said. "She stole my cottage," he went on. "I signed it over to her, and then she came with the deed, Bibi Wolff, Proprietor, and I had to go."

Robert was startled. "Bibi Wolff?"

"That was her name. Bibi Wolff."

"But that's the name of the woman I'm going to marry. Bibi Wolff," Robert said. "And I've signed my cottage over to her."

"It must be a different Bibi Wolff," James began, but before he could go on, there was a knock at the door.

"Who's that?" Robert asked.

The door opened and a very blonde head appeared. "It's me," Bibi announced. "I just came to tell you that I'm leaving you for another man. And I'm going to need the cottage. I want you out by the weekend."

Robert and James looked at each other with a wild surmise. But of course Bibi's papers were all in order, and they had to leave. They got into their Audis and drove over to Winnipeg

Beach. Brother Bruce greeted them with excitement but refused to listen to their story.

"First you have to hear my great news," he said. "I'm getting married next Wednesday. To the most beautiful girl in the world. I met her at the golf club. Her name's Bibi Wolff."

James and Robert shouted out her name in unison. Then they demanded large glasses of scotch, and they told Bruce the story. He admitted that he too had signed his cottage over to her but had not yet given her the deed. She was coming to pick it up that very evening. The three Hoag brothers had not got rich by accident. Together, they formulated a plan, and that evening, when a knock came at the door, they were ready.

"Let me in, Bruce," Bibi called. "I've come for the deed."

Bruce didn't open the door, but he answered in a muffled voice. "I'm sorry, Bibi. I've got a bad case of hay fever. It's all that goldenrod blooming. I've got to stay in my armchair. Doctor's orders."

"But the deed?" Bibi shouted back. "If we're going to get married on Wednesday, I need the deed to show the banker so that I can get the money to pay for my wedding dress!"

"I can't get out of my chair," Bruce answered. "I also have a broken leg. But there is one way. The skylight is open. If you can climb on the roof and lean over through the skylight as far as you can, I might be able to pass it to you."

"That's ridiculous!" Bibi said, and you could hear the anger in her voice.

"Nevertheless, it's the only way," Bruce told her. "There's a ladder leaning up against the shed."

There was a moment of silence, but finally Bibi answered, "Oh, all right." Then the three Hoag brothers heard the sound of someone climbing up the roof. The skylight opened and a pale but beautiful arm reached into the room.

"I'm leaning over as far as I can," Bibi said. "Pass me the deed."

"Just an inch more," Bruce told her, and he brushed her fingertips with the paper. Bibi leaned further into the room, and she fell with a scream and a very large splash right into the hot tub. The Hoag brothers immediately turned the thermostat up to nine, the highest setting, and they didn't let her out of the tub until she signed the cottages back to the brothers. When the police came by, the brothers said it was a crying shame how young women these days got drunk and unruly, but what could you do? The police asked several questions, but after a while they went away.

The brothers sold all three cottages to a German investor and made a huge profit. Then one of them took up sky diving, and another took up car racing and the third took up alligator wrestling, and they risked their lives in sensible ways. But they never married, and they grew old and fat and very, very happy.

THE MAN WHO SAW
BEAUTY EVERYWHERE

obert was driving north on Pembina Highway when he realized that he was weeping. To be more exact, he was at the corner of Pembina and Crane. A little girl in a blue dress danced clumsily in front of her mother, and the moment was so intensely beautiful that Robert burst into tears. It was an embarrassing moment, and Robert checked quickly to see if anyone had noticed, but the drivers of the only cars near him, an older woman in a red Chevette and a young Chinese man in a Trans Am, seemed engrossed in their own concerns.

Robert wiped his eyes with a Kleenex and drove on. Nothing was any different when he got home that night. His wife was late, but she had warned him that she'd be late. Edith was taking a new fitness course at the spa. Robert mixed himself a scotch as he always did when he came home and went out on the deck to drink it. After a minute, he remembered that he'd agreed to start dinner. He went back into the kitchen and found three chicken breasts in a plastic bag in the refrigerator. He put them into a pan, put the pan in the oven and turned the temperature up to 350 degrees. Then he went back

43

to the deck to drink his scotch and look at the roses. The roses were deep red and velvety, but a little bit vulgar.

He was still there on the deck, waiting for the last ice cube to melt so that he could taste the thin, final drop of scotch, when his wife arrived. He had expected her to come through the house and out the back door, but she had come around the side of the house instead, and so he didn't see her until she spoke to him.

"Did you put on the supper?" she asked.

"Yes," Robert replied. "Chicken."

His wife looked beautiful standing there with her new haircut making her look a little like a flapper, wearing the yellow sweater and white pants that he liked so much because they showed off her long legs. Robert realized again that he was weeping, though his wife didn't seem to notice. He pretended that something had got into his eye, and wiped it with the Kleenex, which had got a little balled up after the last use, and which had been torn by the keys in his pocket so that it looked all ratty.

"How was the spa?" he asked his wife.

"Fine," she said. "It's a spa."

"What kind of equipment do they have?"

"The same equipment that spas always have. Bicycles and weights and things."

"What about the people," he asked. "What kind of people were there?"

"What's with the third degree?" she asked him. "I went to the spa. There were other people there exercising. Don't you believe me?"

"Yes," he said. "I believe you."

"Then lay off. I'm tired of being grilled about every detail of my life." His wife went into the house through the sliding glass doors that led from the deck to the kitchen. Robert waited a minute, then followed. His wife was already on the telephone when he got in. When she saw him, she went around the corner and muttered something Robert couldn't hear, then hung up.

The next day, as Robert was driving to work, he noticed that the radio was on a country and western station. Edith must have changed stations when she went out shopping the night before. He was about to change back to the classical music station when he was caught by the words of the song. The singer, a woman, mourned that she would still wait for her unfaithful lover, hoping that he would return even though he had treated her badly. Her song seemed to Robert so full of pathos, so true to the hopeless nature of love and the fragility of the world that he found his eyes full of tears again.

It occurred to Robert that he was losing his sanity. He remembered that breaking into tears was a sure sign that your nerves were bad and that you needed treatment. He didn't feel like he was ill, though. He felt instead as if the world had slowed down just an infinitesimal degree, and he was getting glimpses of things he had never seen before. For a moment he took a kind of pride in his sensitivity. He thought he might write a poem or something, but when he tried to find words for his experiences they seemed hopeless.

During the following week, the tears flowed with a slowly increasing intensity: a pair of lovers, a baby robin, a mother and child and of course his wife. The curve of her hip, the tiny wrinkle of her nose when she laughed, the slight awkwardness that was obvious in everything she did, all of her gestures seemed to him marvels, and he took deep joy in the fact that she was his wife. When he tried to tell her of this, she warned him not to suffocate her.

At work, Robert's colleagues began to be concerned about him. They asked whether anything was wrong. They said he looked as if he needed a holiday. Robert told them, no, he felt fine, he'd just been working too hard for a little while, but he was taking it easier now. They seemed to want him to be more normal, and when he left work that night he felt as if he'd escaped. He had begun to think of his response to beauty as a gift.

Then, one night at a party at the Empsons', he realized that his wife was having an affair. She was talking to a man he had never seen before, a man who looked as if he might have been a football player in his youth. Jill Empson had just announced that the steaks were ready on the barbecue out back, and come help yourselves. The man gently touched Robert's wife on the back, directing her toward the door. The touch was so proprietorial, the response so practiced and familiar that Robert was left without a doubt.

Robert felt very certain that something monumental was about to happen. He had never seriously entertained the notion of his wife's infidelity before, and it seemed to him that a rent had opened in the universe. Outside, under the Empsons' elms she introduced the man to Robert. His name was Leif. He was a Norwegian who owned a construction company. It was he, or at least his men, who had renovated Robert's kitchen. He was coming next week to look at Robert's shingles.

Robert's wife left them and went to refresh her drink. The man was quite talkative, and Robert was pleased to discover that he was silly. The man seemed accustomed to power and to having people believe what he said. He told how he had come over as a stowaway and how he would have been sent back had not the prime minister himself intervened. A little later that evening the talk turned to strange powers, and the man told everyone that he could remember things that had happened while he was still in his mother's womb. Robert feigned great interest, and asked a number of questions. The man found himself making larger and larger claims to special powers, and by the time he realized what Robert was doing, he was red in the face and belligerent. On the way back in the car, Edith was furious. She knew exactly what Robert had done, and she would not forgive him.

"Why did you have to humiliate him?" she asked. "He's a sweet guy. Maybe he can remember things he heard before he was born. You don't know."

"Any maybe cows can fly," Robert told her. "I think I'll get another estimate on the shingles."

And he did. The new estimate was nearly a thousand dollars cheaper than the Norwegian's price, and Robert phoned and cancelled the arrangements his wife had made. She was furious, but she didn't actually say anything. She just stormed around the house for an hour or so, then drove off without saying anything.

Robert went to his wife's desk and began to look through her papers. It was something he had never done before, but it somehow seemed perfectly legitimate now. If his wife was unfaithful to him, then all the rules had changed. And if by some miracle she were not, and he could find evidence of her innocence, then that too was a justification.

In all, it took him about an hour to read everything in her desk, and by the time he was through, he had come to realize the complexity of detective work. If his wife was guilty, then he had overwhelming evidence of it in her notes, strange cryptic entries that said things like N for lunch Tues. 2:00 Bedroom??? If she were innocent, however, every note could be explained. They had talked about adding on a section to the bedroom, and she might simply have discussed it with the contractor. In fact, he remembered now that she had done that very thing, and they had decided it was too expensive.

If she were innocent, then every note, every entry, had to have its own explanation. If she were guilty, on the other hand, then one explanation would do for them all. An assumption of her guilt, like the best scientific theories, had the advantage of simplicity and clarity. Robert walked out into the yard to await his wife's return. A spider had built a web from the lilac to the railing on the deck, and Robert marvelled at its beauty, its simplicity and its clarity. He watched it for a long time, and realized that he felt no emotion. He was not moved to tears as he had been for the past few weeks.

He was struck then that perhaps his strange sensitivity had been related to his wife's infidelity. Perhaps he had somehow realized all along that she was betraying him, and his sadness had expressed itself in that way.

When his wife came home he looked at her out of his new wisdom. She was still as beautiful as ever, but his heart was no longer moved by seeing her. He could think of her in another man's arms without any discomfort. He wondered whether he hated her now, but even that wasn't the case. He simply didn't care. If she was having an affair then that was simply the case, and he would have to take whatever rational steps there were in such a circumstance.

The next day he felt oddly happy. He joked with the people at work, and several of them commented on how he seemed in better health than he had been for a long time. Still, he phoned home several times to see if his wife was at home. A couple of times he hung up as if he had got a wrong number, and once he asked her to look up an address for him. At two-fifteen there was no answer, so he left the office, got into his car and drove home. The garage door was open, and his wife's car was gone.

He calculated his best chance of finding her. She did not know of his suspicions, so she would not yet have taken precautions. He guessed that she would meet the Norwegian for a drink at a bar that was halfway between their house and the Norwegian's office. That would be Clancy's in the mall by the drugstore. The Norwegian's truck was parked there when he arrived, but his wife's car was not. He drove slowly through the parking lot, then circled the block. Still nothing. On an impulse, he turned down the back lane, and there it was, a little red Honda parked behind the bank. Things were happening a little faster than he expected. She had already begun to be careful.

He parked his car in front of the drugstore and went in to buy some aspirins. The clerk was slow serving him, and when he came out the Norwegian's truck was gone. He looked into the bar, but there was nobody there, and when he drove down the lane again, his wife's car was gone.

When he got home, his wife confronted him. She had seen his car parked at the drugstore in the middle of the afternoon. She'd met Leif for a drink to try to explain about the shingles. If she hadn't promised to pick up her mother, she would have waited to find out what was wrong.

"Aspirins," he told her, "only aspirins." He had them in his pocket.

"They don't have aspirins any closer to work than that?" she asked. "Nobody at work could lend you an aspirin?"

"I didn't feel well. I was going to come home and go to bed, but I guess the fresh air helped. I went back to work." He didn't ask her why her car was parked in the back lane. She would have a reason, and he would have to explain why he had been driving down the lane himself.

The next morning, driving to work, Robert noticed that the city had begun to decay. Stucco that should have been white was turning yellow. Everywhere, there were cracks in the concrete foundations of buildings. Paint was peeling from the trim around windows, and everywhere, bits of garbage were blown into hedges and fences.

He continued to check on his wife at every opportunity. He didn't want to take too much time off his work, but almost every day he found her car parked somewhere, never quite hidden, but never just parked in front of wherever she was visiting. And of course he bumped into her accidentally in this way.

"Don't you ever stay in your office and do any work?" she asked him. He had his answers ready. There was always a reason.

He began to look at his wife more critically too. She was nearly forty. Someone had told him that at forty a woman loses either her face or her figure. His wife was losing her figure. In spite of all the time she spent at the spa, her waist had perceptibly thickened. Her body had sagged into itself in a way that he could not explain. There was no single detail in which she had begun to fail, but the overall effect was that she was getting old.

His own new outlook on life did not go unnoticed at the office. Robert was the chief financial officer for the organization and it was his responsibility to see that money wasn't wasted. He checked the accounts of the entire sales force, with the same assiduousness that he had applied to his wife's papers. When he began with the assumption that the salespeople were cheating on their invoices, he discovered corruption everywhere. Several people were fired, the rules were tightened, and Robert was given a raise. All the evidence had been there before, but when he had assumed that people were honest, he had failed to see it.

One day when he came home early and eased himself into the house as quietly as he could, he caught his wife on the telephone. She was saying, in a low voice, "I'm sure he suspects something. I think we better cool it for a while." It was the final piece of evidence he needed, and he confronted her directly with all the sarcasm he could gather.

"And just what needs cooling?" he asked her.

"The salad," she answered. "Have you forgotten about the surprise birthday party for your brother Tom?"

He had indeed forgotten. He didn't much like his brother Tom, and he liked him even less now that he had given Edith a perfect excuse.

"Really, I don't know what's gotten into you," she said. "You walk around as if you had some enormous guilty secret."

And he did have a guilty secret, though he hadn't had it for long. After the crackdown on the salespeople, Robert wasn't as popular as he had been. Still, one of the receptionists, a woman named Cynthia, who had just recently separated from her husband, had shown an interest in him. In fact, she had brazenly asked him out for a drink after work one day. The company frowned on office romance, but he went anyway. On the old adage that what's sauce for the goose is sauce for the gander, he asked her to sleep with him, and she agreed.

Now, confronted with his wife's accusation, he was outraged. "If there are any guilty secrets around this place," he told her, "they're yours."

But, Robert discovered, it was easier to start an affair than to end one. He didn't actually like Cynthia very much. She talked too much, and she had a habit of continually saying aha with a rising inflection, as if what you had just said was the answer to a question she had long pondered. She used it after everything that Robert said, and it was particularly annoying

50

in the office when they were supposed to be working.

More to keep her quiet than anything else, Robert became an assiduous lover. They had to conduct their affair in brief meetings in motel rooms during lunch hour. Cynthia's ex-husband, it turned out, was spying on them, so they had to keep changing motels. He was a mailman, a ridiculous figure in his mailman's shorts trying to see through the motel window with binoculars from across the street.

Because their time was so brief, Robert devoted all his energy to guaranteeing Cynthia's pleasure. She had never been made love to with quite the thoroughness that Robert provided. Certainly not by the mailman. In the office in the afternoon, she actually glowed as if she were lit up from inside. And of course everybody noticed.

Then, of course, everything happened at once. It always does. The owner of the company called Robert into this office and fired him. He was a deeply religious man, and he found Robert's conduct with Cynthia unacceptable. He was grateful for Robert's efficient work, but he could not countenance adultery. There would be a handsome severance package, but there could be no further discussion of the issue.

When he met Cynthia at the motel at noon, she gave him an ultimatum. Either he left his wife and married her, or it was over. She had already called Edith and they had discussed the matter. Robert couldn't bear the thought of a lifetime of ahas, and he said farewell.

As he was leaving the motel, Cynthia's ex and several of his mailman buddies confronted Robert. The mailman accused Robert of ruining his life, and he hit Robert, quite hard in the head. Robert fell to the ground, and some of the other mailmen kicked him while he was down. Fortunately, the motel owner ran out with a baseball bat and chased the mailmen away. Robert slipped into his car and drove home.

Edith was waiting for him. She had packed his clothes, and his suitcases were sitting on the front steps. Robert could see that the big Norwegian contractor was already sitting in an armchair, reading the paper. He took his suitcases, limped back to his car, and drove back to the motel. He had already paid for the whole day.

On his way to the motel, he noticed that all the buildings seemed to have been newly painted. Two little boys, dark-skinned and fine-boned, stood waiting for a light, hand in hand. The younger brother looked up with worship into the eyes of the older, and Robert was so filled with joy at this sign of fraternal love that his eyes filled with tears.

Later, in the divorce court, he was stunned by his ex-wife's beauty, by the grace of her movements. She had not lost her figure after all. And Cynthia, when she returned him his tooth-brush, seemed like some stray goddess, far beyond his reach. He did get his job back. He asked for mercy, and the Christian owner could not refuse him. The world stayed beautiful. But though he lived for a very long time, nothing ever happened to him again.

EYE, EAR, NOSE & THROAT

here was once a young doctor, an eye, ear, nose and throat specialist, who lived in Winnipeg with his ailing mother and his arthritic father. He was good at his profession, and many an eye, ear, nose and throat in Winnipeg owed its comfort to his ministrations. He lived in a small mansion on Wellington Crescent, not because he was interested in material things, but because he was a doctor, and it was expected of him.

Now it came to pass that one day he was called before the College of Physicians and Surgeons to explain his billing practices.

"It appears," said the senior physician who presided at such events, "that you have averaged one hundred and fourteen patients per day for the past seven years without taking a single holiday. Can you explain this unusual fact for us?"

The young doctor blushed. "I do work very hard," he said, "but I hadn't realized that I had put in so many hours. I know that it is unseemly for a doctor to work so hard, but I have never taken an interest in golf." He let his gaze sweep over the College of Physicians and Surgeons, rank on rank of august medical professionals in their white lab coats. They stared back at him sternly.

"I could try again," he suggested. "I could take lessons from the pro at the John Blumberg municipal course, and I could take a winter golf holiday in Texas every year." Even this did not seem to soften them.

"There are serious irregularities in your billings," the senior physician went on. "A single nose, belonging to one Mabel Schwartz of 411 Balfour Drive, has cost the taxpayers of this province over thirty thousand dollars, and it has not as yet received any surgery. What do you have to say for yourself?"

The young doctor felt he was now on surer ground. He explained his philosophy of medicine, how he felt that, since the eye, ear, nose and throat were clustered around the brain, he was as much a psychiatrist as a surgeon. He described the numerous hours he had spent trying to convince Ms Schwartz that her nose worked, that it was pretty, and that she did not require cosmetic surgery.

"I attempted to prevent unnecessary medical procedures," he told the collected College of Physicians and Surgeons with some pride. "But I have recently learned that an operation was performed on her by an unscrupulous plastic surgeon in Saskatoon."

"You have billed the same patient as many as fourteen times for the same procedure," the chief physician went on, ignoring the young doctor's idealistic outburst. "You sometimes bill the same patient three times in a single day for the same procedure."

"I do not send out the bills," the young doctor said with dignity. "That function is performed by my receptionist, Miss Debby Propinski. If that is the source of your concern, then you must speak to her."

The College of Physicians and Surgeons was without sympathy. They took away his license for one year and ordered him to pay back two hundred and seventy-five thousand dollars to the Manitoba Health Insurance Commission. The young doctor was, of course, distraught, but he was a man of resources. He sold his mansion on Wellington Crescent so that he could pay back the government, and he sold his Ferrari and used the money to put his ailing mother and his arthritic father into a nursing home, and he set out to find a wife.

He had never found time before to get himself a wife. In fact, he had not realized that it was his responsibility. He thought that, if he waited, one would come along. He had worked so hard in medical school and in his practice that he failed to discover how courtship was accomplished.

Now he looked around and noticed that doctors invariably married their receptionists. Unfortunately, Miss Debby Propinski was engaged to marry a very large truck driver. In fact, it was they who had purchased both his mansion on Wellington Crescent and his Ferrari.

And so, one bright day in June, the young doctor found himself standing on the Trans Canada Highway, just west of Winnipeg, with nothing but the clothes he was wearing, his little black bag (which he couldn't bear to part with, even though he could no longer practise medicine in Manitoba), and a Visa card with a limit of thirty thousand dollars.

He stood for a long time, hitchhiking first west and then east, and then west again. Finally, he was picked up by an Allied Van Lines furniture truck that was heading west to Regina.

The driver was very friendly. "Where are you going, young feller?" he asked.

"I'm going to find myself a wife," the young doctor confessed. "I worked so hard at my studies and my practice that I neglected to find one, and now I must marry before I grow too old."

"Well, you're heading in the right direction," the truck driver said. "The best wives in all the country are to be found in the west, if only you know where to look for them. I could tell you the exact spot, but that spot is a secret, known only to the members of the Furniture Van Driver's Guild, and I have vowed a mighty oath of secrecy."

The young doctor begged the truck driver to tell him the location, but the truck driver refused.

"A van driver's oath is a powerful oath, and I wouldn't want to take a chance on breaking it."

The young doctor noticed then that they were going very fast. The truck veered from side to side, and several times they were nearly struck by other vehicles. By the time they hit the Saskatchewan border, the young doctor was guiding the truck driver's every move, telling him to move now right, now left, watch out for the parked car, slow down for the radar trap. Finally, just across the border, the truck driver stopped.

"I can go no further," he said. "I have to confess that my eyesight has failed so that I can no longer see the road. I will have to resign from the Furniture Van Driver's Guild and make my living begging for crusts of bread in the Regina bus depot." And he burst into tears.

"Nonsense," the young doctor told him. "Medical science can easily cure your problem, and I would gladly help you, but that my license to practise in Manitoba has been cancelled."

"We're not in Manitoba," the truck driver said. "We're in Saskatchewan. That town just before us is Indian Head."

"Why, you're right," the young doctor cried. "Quick, step outside." He took an eye chart out of his little black bag, nailed it to the side of the truck and asked the truck driver to read it. The truck driver could only read the big E. He couldn't even see the line that goes SNVRT. Quickly, the young doctor wrote down a prescription and handed it to the truck driver. The truck driver took the prescription, walked in to Indian Head to an optician's shop and returned an hour later with a pair of glasses. He could see perfectly now, and he drove slowly and courteously all the rest of the way to Regina.

Just as the driver let the young doctor out at the bypass around Regina, he said, "You have saved my job, and by so doing you have saved my life. Now I will not have to beg for scraps in the Regina bus depot. The Furniture Van Driver's Code permits me to tell you a secret under these conditions. The best wives in all of Canada are to be found in Rossland, British Columbia." And he drove off, leaving the young doctor with nothing but the smell of diesel fumes and a direction for his quest.

A few minutes later, a Reimer's Express furniture van stopped, and the driver waved him aboard.

"Thank you," the young doctor said. "I am on my way to Rossland, British Columbia to find myself a wife. Are you by any chance going in that direction?"

The driver did not reply. He didn't even turn to look at the young doctor.

"I said, 'Are you going all the way to Rossland, B.C.?' "

There was still no reply.

"Are you going to Rossland?" the young doctor shouted.

Finally, the driver turned to him. "No," he said. "I'm already married."

The young doctor saw what was the matter. He indicated to the driver that he should pull into an Esso station in Moose Jaw, and the driver did. Then the young doctor took a vial from his little black bag, and he put one drop into each of the driver's ears. He wrote out a prescription and allowed the driver to keep the rest of the sample he had used.

The driver was ecstatic. Miraculously, he could hear again. The young doctor told him all about his quest for a wife, and the driver said, "You have saved my job, and very likely my life. If I should fail to pass the hearing test that the Motor Vehicles Branch has scheduled for Thursday, I would surely lose my license and have to beg for scraps of food in the Calgary bus depot. Because you have saved my life, the Furniture Van Driver's Code permits me to tell you one secret. When you get to Rossland, go directly to the Esso service station and ask for Dave. He will tell you how to find the perfect wife."

The driver let the young doctor out in Medicine Hat. He caught a ride to Lethbridge with a Mennonite lay minister, who cautioned him on the dangers of women from the Kootenays. From Lethbridge to Pincher Creek he rode with a bookstore manager, who told him erotic tales about the women from the Kootenays. Just outside Crow's Nest Pass he was picked up by an ex-hockey player from the Trail Smoke Eaters, who drove him all the way to Rossland. The streets of Rossland were filled with beautiful women. They moved singly or in pairs, though sometimes there were groups of as many as four or five. Many of them seemed to be dressed for skiing, though it was still mid-June, and several of them were eating Mars Bars. The young doctor was tempted to stop and make their acquaintance, but he remembered the furniture van driver's advice, and he went directly to Dave's Esso. Dave was there, a man of about three hundred pounds with the reddest nose the young doctor had ever seen. He blew it constantly, and he sneezed and coughed. When the young doctor explained his quest, Dave was not sympathetic.

"You think it's easy," he said, sniffing and coughing. "You can just come to Rossland and get a wife. Well, there are barely enough wives to go around for the men of Rossland, what with all the single guys down at the Cominco smelter in Trail. Get yourself a wife at home, and leave the Kootenay women alone."

The young doctor saw what he must do. He took a package of antihistamine tablets from his little black bag and gave one to Dave. Dave was suspicious, but he swallowed the pill and in minutes he was entirely cleared up, and his nose was no longer red.

"Thank you," said Dave. "For thirty years I have suffered from this allergy, and I have not drawn a single breath in comfort. Now I am cured. Because you have done me this great favour, the Esso Service Station Operator's Code permits me to tell you one secret. The most perfect wives are to be found sleeping in glass coffins near the top of Red Mountain. But be careful. If you try to wake one and fail, she will die, and you will never have a wife."

The young doctor set off eagerly for Red Mountain. The resort was closed for the summer, but he walked straight up the very steep slope of the mountain. By the time he had reached halfway, he was nearly exhausted and he had begun to wonder whether he needed a wife at all. By the time he was near the top, he would gladly have given up his quest. Then suddenly, he came upon a glass coffin. A very pretty dark-haired girl was sleeping in it. The young doctor was just about to kiss her and awaken her when he noticed a slightly grim set about her lips.

"No," he thought, "this is not the wife for me. She seems too set in her ways."

A hundred yards higher up the mountain was another glass coffin. An even prettier redhead slept there, but just as he was about to kiss her and awaken her, a quick frown of anger slipped across her face.

"No," the young doctor thought, "I do not want a wife who will always be angry with me and make my life miserable."

Right at the very top of the mountain, he came upon a third glass coffin. Here slept the most beautiful girl he had ever seen, dressed in an attractive skiing outfit. She had golden hair that curled around her neck in ringlets. Her eyes were green, her ears were like tiny oysters, and her nose was smooth and perfect. The young doctor leaned over and kissed her.

Nothing happened. The young woman lay as still as if she were dead.

Suddenly the young doctor remembered his medical training. He pulled her to a sitting position and applied the Heimlich manoeuvre. A chunk of apple came out of her throat, and she began to breathe freely. The young doctor gave her an aspirin from his little black bag, and in no time she was feeling fine. They were married that very day, and the young doctor gave her the Visa card with the thirty thousand dollar limit. He decided to give up medicine and, even though the bank reduced the Visa limit to thirty-five hundred when they found out that he was no longer a doctor, they are both very happy. They have three beautiful daughters, and it is expected that each will win an Olympic gold medal in her turn.

LAMB'S LETTUCE

apunzel, Rapunzel, let down your hair. This is the cry of the witch. The witch wants only to preserve beauty and innocence. The mother's greed, the father's cowardice, these are the roots of the problem. Lamb's lettuce, the mother cries, I must have lamb's lettuce.

What can a father do, there in the high-walled garden? He must give his unborn daughter to the witch. The child may not be a daughter, there may not be a birth, nothing is certain. What is the promise of an unborn daughter worth? A handful of lamb's lettuce.

Later of course there is the high tower, the fair maiden combing her hair. Rapunzel, Rapunzel, let down your hair. This is the cry of the witch, her black rags flapping like a crow. And the golden hair tumbling from the window, spilling from the high window. The witch is up it in a minute, full of cautions, full of warnings for the fair maiden with the golden hair. The witch loves beauty and innocence. Who can blame her for wanting to preserve it? The maiden answers yes mother to the witch. She cannot know the shadowy negotiations of the past, her mother's greed, her father's cowardice.

Then must come the inevitable prince, son of the king, ravisher of maidens. The witch is out. She has gone on a journey. The prince in his slyness has listened from the forest. And what can we watchers do? The witch is too far away for us to call her. Rapunzel, Rapunzel, let down your hair, the king's son calls, and the innocent hair tumbles free. Now the prince is ascending, he enters the window, and we below can do nothing. What chance has Rapunzel against the smooth tongue of a prince? How can a young girl remember cautions when her guardians are absent?

When the witch returns, she understands in a moment. There is a knowing look in the eye of the girl. She has knowledge that is hard to come by in a lonely tower in the forest. The witch is maddened with rage, she is sick with grief. She cuts off Rapunzel's hair, a hopeless gesture. It will only grow again. She sends Rapunzel to a desert place. When the prince, despoiler of innocence, arrives again, she is ready. When he calls Rapunzel, Rapunzel, let down your hair, the witch flings her hair out the window. When the prince reaches the window, she casts him to the ground, where his eyes are put out by the thorns on the bramblebush where he falls. Then the witch weeps for lost innocence, her black heart breaking for the beauty that has been tarnished, for the death that has entered the world. She is weeping still.

But that's not the end of the story. There is more to come. There are the seven years of wandering, Rapunzel with the twins, a boy and a girl, the fruit of her one mad hour. At last they meet again, Rapunzel and the prince. She weeps tears of joy, crystal tears that fall on the prince's eyelids, and he sees again. They return to his kingdom where they grow fat in a period of slow peace. The daughter is sold for a handful of lamb's lettuce. The son becomes a famous ravisher of innocent maidens.

THE HARDWARE
DEALER'S DAUGHTER

he owner of the hardware store in Maple River was wealthy beyond the envy of his neighbours, from Willow Creek right on north to Howardsville. He had built up his business from scratch, and in those early days his neighbours had envied him. But then his father had died back in England and left him four hundred thousand pounds and a castle, and he had never even met his father. His mother had brought him to Canada when he was two and had told him his father had died in the war, though now that he thought about it, she had never mentioned what war. The British government was taking taxes from the estate to pay for the castle at what seemed like an alarming rate, and the owner of the hardware store supposed he'd have to go to England soon and do something about it. Sell the castle probably.

But then his wife's father had also died, and it turned out that he had owned the biggest cat food factory in Canada. Once, he had been charged with selling tainted tuna to cat owners all over North America. His picture had even been in the *Maple River Herald,* but Mary hadn't even mentioned it because she was ashamed of her father for doing things like that. Anyway, he left them five million dollars, the cat food factory and a professional ping-pong team consisting of five Chinese players who were on a continual around-the-world tour.

Then he won a lottery, ten thousand dollars on a scratch-and-win ticket that he'd bought at the Husky station in Gimli when they stopped for gas the time they went to the hardware store owner's convention at the new hotel there. After that, nobody envied him. They only wanted to be his friend.

It happened that the hardware store owner had a beautiful daughter. She had recently completed a master's degree in English at the University of Toronto, but times were hard, and she couldn't get a job anywhere. She decided to come back to Maple River and work in the hardware store. Her father hadn't mentioned the wealth he had recently acquired, because it was an awkward topic to bring up, and he didn't want his daughter to think badly of him. She had been in the student NDP party in high school, and at the time she had disapproved of wealth. Her letters home from Toronto had begun to suggest that she might have changed her mind, but her father wasn't certain. His motto had always been "better safe than sorry," and he invoked it now.

The daughter had been named Kimberly even before anyone knew she might inherit a castle. Kimberly Clark. Her father had found the name on a carton of paper towels and suggested it to her mother, who had not objected, and as far as the hardware store owner knew, no one had ever noticed. She had scarcely returned from Toronto before the suitors began to arrive.

The first of her suitors was a mountie named Dave. He confessed to the hardware store owner that he had spent some time with Kimberly in the back seat of the patrol car out at Foster's Lake, and he offered to do the decent thing and marry her. The hardware store owner brought the proposal to his daughter, but she only laughed. She said that Dave the Mountie had the conversational skills of a grapefruit and that his only courtship manoeuvre was the slap shot. She wouldn't marry him even if the only alternative was a farmer.

The second suitor was a curler from Sioux Lookout named Lorne. He confessed that he had spent some time in a motel with Kimberly at the cash bonspiel in Portage la Prairie. He brought his entire team to testify to his love, and they all agreed that, ever since the skip had met Kimberly, their game had collapsed. They lost out in the zone finals, and didn't even get a shot at the Brier. Kimberly said that Lorne gave the word "hog-line" a whole new meaning, and even if life went to an extra end, she wouldn't marry him.

The third suitor was a CBC television reporter named Harvey. He was in town doing a story about the new hog operation just east of town that the Hutterites had started. He had red hair and a thin ethereal build. He confessed to the hardware store owner that he had spent a passionate hour with Kimberly after the winter carnival, at which, incidentally, Kimberly had won the title of Winter Queen, because her father had purchased nine thousand dollars worth of tickets. Kimberly said she wouldn't marry Harvey to save the free world. She said he had the aesthetic judgement of a turnip and the athletic grace of a slug.

Then the hardware store owner knew that his daughter's long study of English literature had hardened her heart. One evening when she was out at bingo with her mother, he went to her room and looked at her bookshelf. There he found books on deconstruction and postmodernism and filthy books of poetry that failed to observe the left-hand margin. Treatises on feminism were everywhere, and she had even surreptitiously joined the League of Canadian Poets as an associate member. The hardware store owner knew what he would have to do.

He called his daughter into the kitchen. "Kimberly," he said, "I have not mentioned this to you before because I thought you would disapprove, but now I see that I must. I have untold riches that you must inherit, and before I die, I want to see you properly cared for. To that end, I have advertised in the newspapers so that all the eligible men in the country may vie for your hand. You must propose a riddle, and whosomever shall answer your riddle shall be your husband."

Kimberly pointed out to her father that the word "whomsoever" had not been used since the early nineteenth century and, furthermore, if she were to inherit untold wealth, the last thing she wanted was a husband. A husband, she said, ranked right there behind a vacuum cleaner as an object of desire. When he refused to relent, she moved to Regina without leaving a forwarding address, but her father used his untold wealth to hire Herman's Private Detective Service out of Winnipeg to find her. In short order, Herman discovered her working in the last discotheque in North America, subdued her with chloroform, and took her off to England and locked her in a tower of the castle. There she brooded on the cruelties of fate, and tried to frame a riddle that would guarantee her the least offensive husband out of the trail of nerds she expected.

And of course suitors came from every country in the world. They paid their own way and stayed in local hotels or camped out on the grounds of the castle. The traffic was so heavy that questions were raised in the British House of Commons about the number of foreigners entering England. But Kimberly had set cruel conditions for those who would aspire to her hand. Anyone could attempt to answer the riddle, but he would have to sign a contract that if he failed he would agree to be retrained as an accountant and assigned to work as a junior partner in an accountancy firm in Guelph, Ontario. In the end, though thousands had gathered, only three were brave enough to risk the consequences of vying for Kimberly's hand.

The first was a gigantic Turk with a huge bristly moustache and cruel eyes. He was dressed only in a pair of harem pants and he brandished a scimitar.

"I am afraid of nothing," he cried, and he waved the scimitar around his head and cursed a mighty Turkish curse. Kimberly thought he was cute, but her will had been hardened by a course in eighteenth-century women's literature at the

University of Toronto and she didn't flinch. Her question was ready. One summer she had worked for a Toronto firm that designed skill-testing questions for cereal companies that wished to give away Chrysler Le Barons to anyone who would cut out the form on the back of the box and send it or a reasonable facsimile thereof along with proof of purchase to Box 1172, Station A, Downsview, Ontario. She knew that no one had ever won a Chrysler Le Baron and been able to claim it. Thousands of the shiny vehicles were rusting in a private lot out in Mississauga, because no one could answer the question.

She asked it now.

"What is 7 times 9 plus 141, divided by 2 less 102?"

A look of panic came into the Turk's eyes.

"May I use a calculator?" he asked.

"No."

"May I have a pen and a piece of paper?"

"No."

"How much time have I got?"

"Time's up."

The Turk cursed a mighty Turkish curse, but it was no use. The guards seized him, forced a copy of Forrester's *Basic Principles of Accounting* into his hands and dragged him from the room. He left moaning what seemed to be the Turkish word for "Guelph."

The second suitor was a tall Swedish tennis player. He had golden hair and eyes the colour of robins' eggs. When Kimberly saw him there dressed in his white Reeboks, his white T-shirt and his white shorts, she almost relented. But she had once written a paper on patriarchal domination in the novels of Margaret Laurence, and that had hardened her heart. She asked the question.

"What is 7 times 9 plus 141, divided by 2 less 102?"

A look of panic came into the Swede's eyes.

"May I use a calculator?" he asked.

"No."

"May I have a pen and a piece of paper?"

"No."

"How much time have I got?"

"Time's up."

The tennis player cursed a mighty Swedish curse, but it was no use. The guards seized him, forced a copy of Forrester's *Basic Principles of Accounting* into his hands and dragged him from the room. He left moaning what seemed to be the Swedish word for "Guelph."

The third suitor was a young accountant from Guelph. He was a slight man, prematurely bald, with large horn-rimmed glasses. Kimberly's heart sank with dread. It was clear that this suitor had nothing to lose. She searched her mind desperately for a riddle that might stump him.

"How does Hegel distinguish between *Aufnehemen,* mere "taking up," and *Auffassen,* "apprehending," in the *Phenomenology of Spirit?*

The judges ruled that her question was out of order since it was not an authentic skill-testing question.

"Would you explain how meaning is both deferred and delayed in Derrida's criticism of Saussure's binary notion of the sign?"

The judges ruled that the question was out of order since it was not the kind of question on which a meaningful relationship could be based.

Kimberly realized she was trapped. With a shaking voice she asked the question.

"What is 7 times 9 plus 141, divided by 2 less 102?"

The accountant barely twitched. "Nothing," he said.

"Do you want a calculator?" she asked.

"No."

"Do you want a pen and a piece of paper?"

"No. Time's up. You have to marry me."

And so Kimberly had to go off and live in Guelph with the accountant. They had three beautiful daughters. One was tall and dark and looked Turkish. The other was blue-eyed and golden-haired and looked Swedish. The third looked exactly as Kimberly herself had as a young child.

Kimberly's parents died shortly after that, and left her their untold riches. The first thing she did was take her accountant husband skiing in the Rockies, where he broke his neck on the bunny slope and died instantly. Then she founded a feminist collective in the Queen Charlotte Islands where she lived happily ever after. She passed on her untold wealth to her daughters, but only on the condition that they never marry. And they lived happily ever after too.

ANGEL, BABY

nce upon a time in a small suburb of Winnipeg called Transcona, there lived a husband and a wife. They had two beautiful children, and had decided that two would be sufficient. Then one day, to their surprise, they discovered that another child was on the way, and before they could even make plans, it had arrived, another boy. They decided to love him even though they had not desired him.

Then one day when Carolyn was bathing him, she noticed something odd. There was no doubt about it, she decided. The baby was growing wings. Not that they'd actually sprouted or anything, but when you rolled the baby over on his stomach to powder him, you could see the faint outline of the shape they were going to take. If you laid him down by the window, you could see hundreds of tiny feathers just below the skin.

"Come here, Randy," she told her husband one night about a week after she'd first noticed the feathers. "Look at the baby."

"He could use a diaper," Randy replied. "I know everything about a baby is so sweet that you're supposed to love it, but frankly, naked bottoms are not my cup of tea, if you know what I mean."

"But don't you notice anything strange?" she asked. "Isn't there something very odd about the baby?"

Randy looked again. "He's no odder than the other ones were. Tom and Jimmy both looked a little less like a fish than this one does, but none of them were anything to write home about." Randy liked children after they had hair and teeth and could walk. He liked them even better when they could speak. But he'd had little more than a passing acquaintance with his two older sons until they were two years old. Then he grew to love them dearly. He was not particularly interested in getting to know this one while it was only six months old.

"But look carefully," Carolyn said. "Isn't there something very strange about his back?"

"He's got a bit of a rash," Randy said. "And he's got great bony shoulder blades like your aunt Agnes. I hate to disappoint you, but other than that, this fella is pure run-of-the-mill milk-fed baby."

"Doesn't it look like he's growing wings?" Carolyn persisted. "Doesn't it look like one of these days he's going to sprout a pair of wings?"

Randy looked carefully at the baby. He picked him up and tossed him a couple of inches into the air and caught him. "No." he said. "He's not ready to fly yet."

"But Randy, really," Carolyn said. "Look at him really carefully."

Randy looked at her instead. "Are you okay?" he asked. "You're not on Valium or Phenobarbs or anything?"

"No."

"And you haven't been sneaking into the gin?"

"Of course not. You don't have to believe me. But there is something very strange about this baby." And she took the baby from Randy's arms and flounced out of the room.

"He's got a name," Randy shouted out after her. "His name is Michael. We can't just go on calling him 'the baby.'"

Randy was not given to brooding, but the next day at work,

he brooded about his wife. Carolyn was usually pretty level-headed, for which he was grateful, considering that the rest of her family were famous for their eccentricities. Her mother had a paper route and delivered flyers to make extra money, though she had no need for this, since her husband was quite wealthy. Carolyn's father had made his money selling church supplies, candles and altars and vestments, though he himself was a committed Swedenborgian and never attended church. Her brother had been discharged from the army for doing something so outrageous that even the army wouldn't admit what it was. Her only sister made her living jumping out of cakes.

But Carolyn wasn't his only problem. Ames Brothers Software Solutions, the company for which he worked, was down-sizing. There was a staff of ten, nine of whom were related to the Ames brothers. Five people were to be fired and one promoted. Randy was realistic enough to know that he wasn't going to be promoted and had very little chance of escaping the cut.

So when the sleazy looking man in the black suit sidled up to him in the bar across the street from his office, Randy listened to him.

"Randy," the man said, "you are in a tough position. All those mouths to feed and nothing but unemployment insurance to feed them with. And after that it's welfare."

These were pretty much the thoughts that Randy himself had been thinking for the past few days, but all he said was, "What's the deal?"

"It's like this," the man began, drawing on his cigarette and breathing the smoke in Randy's face. "I can get you a piece of the action at Ames Brothers, not only the promotion but a partnership in the whole operation, but in return . . ."

Meanwhile, Carolyn was facing problems of her own. The baby wouldn't eat pabulum any more. The only thing it would eat was milk and honey, and the odd spoonful of rose-petal jelly. The wings were much more noticeable now, even though Randy seemed completely unaware of them. One day when the baby was about ten months old and just starting to take its first steps, it disappeared. Carolyn turned her back for a second, and it was gone. There was nothing but the room where he had been and an open window. She ran through the house searching for him, calling him by name, "Michael, Michael, Michael." She found him in an upstairs bedroom. He appeared to have just flown in through the window.

When Randy came home that evening, she told him, "Michael, we have to talk. Something I don't understand is happening. I might be going crazy."

"Please try not to lose your marbles entirely," Randy said. "It wouldn't be appropriate for the wife of the new partner in Ames, Ames, Ames and Wilson Software Solutions to wander around like Ophelia at the country club, crying out 'here's rue for remembrance.'"

"Randy, what do you mean? I thought you were worried about losing your job."

"Not any more," Randy told her. "I am now a partner and part-owner of the company, and if you'll walk out to the new minivan in the driveway, you'll find a set of golf clubs and a membership in the St. Charles Golf and Country Club."

"But how?"

"Never mind how. Just put on your dancing gown. Tonight we boogie."

"But Randy, I've got to tell you something about the baby."

"Forget the baby. Tonight we celebrate."

And they did. They celebrated with champagne and wine and too many glasses of Cointreau. Susan had to get up with the two older boys because they had to go to school. She had a headache, and her mouth tasted as if she had eaten something rotten. She looked out the window just as she was taking the toast out of the toaster and saw the baby sitting in the top of a tree. It was either the baby or a very large owl. She went to the bookshelf in the living room and got the binoculars, but when she got back, whatever it was had flown away. The baby was asleep in his crib when she went to look for him, but the window was open, and Carolyn did not remember having opened the window. Of course, she couldn't remember how she had got home from the country club either.

Randy had a headache too, and he blinked several times before he recognized the man in the black suit who was sitting behind his desk.

"How did you get in here?" he asked.

"I told your secretary I was from the Underground Fire Control Company, looking for software solutions to keeping our furnaces burning. But let's get to the point. You've got the partnership, a ten-thousand-dollar bonus and a membership in the St. Charles Golf and Country Club?"

"Yes."

"I've kept my part of the bargain."

"Yes."

"Well, then I'll drop around your place later this afternoon to claim your first-born. What time does he get back from school? Around three-thirty?"

Randy thought about his oldest son. Tom was eight and had just got his first two-wheeler.

"You didn't say anything about the first-born," he told the man in the black suit. "You just said a child."

"But surely you know the convention," the man in the black suit said. "It's always the first-born. That's the way it's done."

"Not the first-born." Randy insisted. "That was not part of the agreement." The man took a sheet of paper out of his pocket and studied it.

"Okay," he said. "I'm going to have to change this contract for next time. How about the second-born?"

Randy didn't want to lose Jimmy either. He was just six and in grade one. He was learning to read and was terribly excited to figure out what was written on the sides of cornflakes boxes, especially if it was about dinosaurs. They settled on the baby, and after some argument, they put off the delivery date for a year. Tom knew that Carolyn would be pretty upset, and he wanted to prepare her for the child's disappearance, not that he had any idea how you could prepare someone for something like that.

Meanwhile, Carolyn was having more trouble with the baby. It came and went as it pleased through the open window, and, although it was only a little over a year old, it had learned to read. It read the entire Bible, underlining passages with a red crayon. It had started bringing home library books, though Carolyn couldn't figure out how it got them. Randy was no help. He wouldn't talk about the baby, and he wouldn't change its diaper. He wouldn't even pick it up. She tried to talk to her parents. Her mother gave the baby a subscription to *Owl* magazine, and her father gave her a book by Swedenborg which was incomprehensible.

Then one day, nearly six months after the celebration, the baby began to talk. It began by reciting the Nicene Creed from one end to the other. Then it did Hamlet's soliloquy and sang an aria from *Porgy and Bess*. Finally, it spoke directly to Carolyn.

"Our father is in trouble," it told her. "He's in way over his head."

"What do you mean?" Carolyn asked. "What has he done?" When the baby wasn't talking, it looked just like a baby, but as soon as it spoke it seemed to be eight feet tall.

"You'll find out tomorrow," it said. "But now, I want you to find a farmer's supply store and buy me a set of blacksmith's tongs."

"Blacksmith's tongs?"

"Right."

She bought the tongs and put them in the front hallway in the umbrella stand. When Randy came home she told him, "Randy, this has gone on long enough. We've got to talk about the baby."

"Michael?"

"He's the only baby we've got."

"What about him?"

"Something has got to be done. Michael is not an ordinary baby."

"Well, it doesn't matter," Randy said. "We won't have to worry about him after tomorrow. I sold him."

"You what?"

"I sold him. To a man in a black suit. So that I'd get the partnership and everything." And Randy confessed his entire dealing with the man in the black suit. He even told Carolyn about the rule of the first-born, and how he'd managed to trick the fellow on that one.

"Don't be ridiculous," Carolyn told him. "This is 1994. You can't sell your soul to the devil in 1994."

"I didn't. I sold the baby. Him. Michael."

"You can't sell children either," she told him. "I'm calling the police." And she did call the police, but they weren't at all sympathetic. A couple of men in uniform came to the door and warned them about the charges for public mischief.

That night Randy and Carolyn had a long conversation. They decided that things of the spirit were more important than worldly goods. Carolyn confessed that she hated golf and that the people at the country club were all snobs. The baby was a little strange, but after all, it was their baby, and they had responsibilities.

The next day, the man in the black suit arrived at the door at about two o'clock in the afternoon. The baby was having its afternoon nap in the playpen.

"Well, well. What a fine looking boy," the man said. "This turns out to be a fair deal."

"You can't have him." Carolyn said. "We're not giving him up."

The man looked shocked. He turned to Randy. "I believe we have a deal. Signed in blood as I remember. You can't back out now."

"Carolyn's right," Randy said. "We're not giving him up."

"What about the first-born?"

"Not him either."

"We'll see about that," the man said, and he grabbed the baby out of its playpen and ran out the door. Carolyn noticed that as they passed the umbrella stand, the baby snatched up the blacksmith's tongs.

"Come back," Randy shouted and he ran for the door, but Carolyn stopped him.

"Just wait a minute," she said. "I think it's going to be all right."

Outside the door, the baby had grown ten feet tall. His wings sparkled in the sunlight and his body seemed covered in gold. The man in the black suit looked at him with horror.

"It's a cheat," he cried, "I've been tricked." And he suddenly burst out of his suit to show his horns and his tail and his cleft feet. In only a second, he was thirty feet tall and breathing fire, but not before the baby, Michael, that is, had caught the man's tongue in the blacksmith's tongs and hung on for dear life. The first blast of fire leveled all the houses on the far side of the street. Michael swung the tongs and the man landed on a Taco Bell on the corner, totally demolishing it. The man, who by now seemed to have turned into a dragon, swung Michael so hard that he knocked a pizza delivery van into a ditch. Still he hung on until the whole neighbourhood was charred and burning, and the mall three blocks away was only a deep cavern. Finally, there was a brilliant flash of fire, and the baby was left holding only an old black suit. He threw it into a garbage can and sat down on the doorstep. In a moment, he had stretched out and fallen asleep.

When Carolyn and Randy opened the door a few minutes later, they found the baby sleeping on the doorstep. It was a beautiful day, the sun shining and birds singing. Everything looked exactly normal, except it all seemed cleaner and brighter than it ever had before. The houses on the other side of the street all seemed newly painted. The baby still held the blacksmith's tongs in his tiny hands.

"Wow," Randy said. "We've got a tough kid here."

Carolyn picked up the baby and began to rub his tiny back, on which there was, after all, no sign of wings.

"Don't be silly," she said. "He's only a baby."

THE EVIL
STEPCHILDREN

nce, not so very long ago, a beautiful young woman named Stephanie fell in love with a handsome television anchorman. He had beautiful silver hair and a deep mellifluous voice, and she was half in love with him from the late news before she ever actually met him. She had been married once before to a famous Canadian poet who never washed, but she had got up one morning and found him using her toothbrush, and so she had left him that very day. She didn't count that marriage.

The anchorman had also been married once before. In fact, his wife had left him for the famous Canadian poet who never washed, and Stephanie had met the anchorman in family court at one of those endless hearings that are required to end a modern marriage. The anchorman had two children from his earlier marriage, a boy of fifteen named Hans and a girl of thirteen named Greta. Stephanie promised that she would try to win their affection. She knew she could never replace their mother but thought that with good will on both sides, they might eventually become buddies.

At first, things went reasonably well. The children stayed with their mother while Stephanie and the anchorman went on a honeymoon to Costa Rica where they slept late every morning and went out bird-watching in the afternoons. When they returned, the anchorman still had a couple of weeks of holidays so they lazed around home while the children were at summer camp. Stephanie had kept her job as the design editor for a national women's magazine, and everybody was so busy that they didn't spend much time together until school started in September.

Then one day Greta appeared for breakfast dressed as a teenage hooker. She wore a low-cut white blouse, a short leather skirt, net stockings and high heels. Her eyes were so blackened with mascara that she looked a little like a raccoon, and she wore neon lipstick.

"You're not going to school dressed like that?" Stephanie asked.

"What do you mean?"

"The costume. You can't go to grade seven looking like a tart in a seedy movie."

"What's wrong with this outfit? My mom bought me this. It's what all the girls are wearing." And with that Greta ran from the room in tears. The anchorman followed her, and Stephanie could hear him consoling Greta, talking to her in his low, beautiful voice.

Afterwards, he said to Stephanie, "Could you try to be a bit more sensitive to Greta's needs? She's going through a difficult period. Styles do change you know, and she does want to be like the other kids. Now, she's missed her bus. Would you mind driving her to school?"

Stephanie was so mad she could have spit. She wanted to say that she knew a lot more about styles than he did, thanks. It was how she made her living. And his ex-wife's notion of style had been to cover the walls of the kitchen in green and fuschia flowered wallpaper. But she didn't say anything. She drove Greta to school, and sure enough, all her friends also looked like teenage hookers.

Hans was no better. He burped loudly at the dinner table. He took off his dirty clothes and left them wherever they dropped. He took one-and-one-half-hour showers and used up all the hot water, and he blew his nose loudly into the sink. One night at supper he was apparently trying to suck his soup directly into his body without the aid of a spoon when Stephanie could take no more. She showed him her spoon.

"Do you know what this is?"

"Yeah, it's a spoon."

"Good, now would you take yours, put it into your soup like this, raise it to your mouth, put it all the way into your mouth, close your mouth, and then swallow silently."

"You don't like the way I eat?"

"I don't like the sound of your eating."

"You always criticize me. I can't do nothin' around here. I hate this place. I hate you." He turned to his father. "I hate you, too. If you weren't so mean, Mom wouldn't never have gone." And he ran crying from the room.

The anchorman followed Hans to console him in his deep, lovely voice.

Later the anchorman said to Stephanie, "Look, Steph, the kid's having a rough time. His mother has rejected him entirely. She doesn't mind taking out Greta and buying her clothes, but she doesn't want to have anything to do with Hans. Could you try and be a little sympathetic? He needs a proper relationship with a woman."

He needs a boot in the butt, Stephanie thought, but she didn't say that aloud. She had something in common with the anchorman's ex-wife, she reflected. Neither of them could stand his son. Still, she tried. She asked him to bring over some of his friends. He did so and they sat around all day long, playing Nintendo, squeezing their pimples and giggling. They had burping contests and sneaked into the basement to smoke cigarettes.

Work wasn't going all that well either. There was talk that they were going to be merged with another magazine and they'd only need one design department. The new editor was a committed feminist, and since she'd arrived they'd published articles about why it was dangerous to shave your legs and some tough articles on politics, and the subscription rate had plummeted. Stephanie lived in daily fear that her job would end and she would have to spend full time with the kids.

The kids, meanwhile, had developed new weapons. Stephanie had brought her baby grand piano to the marriage. Greta took to playing it incessantly, the theme from *Star Wars* over and over again. She only played when her fingers were sticky from jam, and after a while, the keys stopped coming up by themselves. Hans begged his father for his own stereo system, which he played so loud that the walls of the house shook. He only played it loud when Stephanie was home. If his father came home, he played it quietly and sensibly. In fact Stephanie could tell when the anchorman was coming home, even if he wasn't expected. Through some sixth sense only available to stepchildren, he always turned down the sound thirty seconds before his father arrived.

"You're much too sensitive to things," the anchorman told Stephanie. "They're just ordinary kids, doing what ordinary kids do. They're not engaged in some sort of conspiracy to drive you mad."

"If they're not," Stephanie thought, "then I'd hate to think what they could do if they tried."

Then one day, the anchorman was sent out to do live reports from Nagorno-Karabach. Stephanie was left with the children for an entire month. They stepped up their war on her sanity. Hans and some of his friends got into the anchorman's liquor cabinet and drank a bottle of single-malt scotch. Then they backed her Toyota Corolla into the neighbour's BMW. Stephanie had to go down to the police station to get them out.

"Your son is very lucky he didn't get into a worse accident," the officer told her. "Some parents are simply irresponsible about the way they handle alcohol, and their children are the victims of their neglect. I hope I don't see your son here again, because the next time the consequences will be much worse." Stephanie took him home and delivered his two drunken friends to their own homes. Each of them vomited in her car, and she considered setting it on fire in the driveway and letting it burn rather than cleaning it.

Then one evening a few days later, Stephanie came home and heard noises from Greta's bedroom, and went in to find Greta lying on the bed with a large hairy boy. They were not actually making love, but the distinction was a fine one. Stephanie ordered the boy out of the house, and he went. The boy was tall, with shifty eyes and he never looked directly at Stephanie. He roared his motorcycle as he left.

"I hate you." Greta screamed at Stephanie. "I can never do anything around here. Now Brad will never come back. Why don't you die, you old witch!" And she ran screaming from the house, out into the dark.

And at that moment, something snapped in Stephanie. She lay awake the whole night making plans. In the morning, she looked normal, except for the hollow stare in her eyes and the unnatural slowness of her movements. She made herself a cup of coffee and drank it slowly. Then she went to Greta's room and knocked on the door.

"What do you want?"

"I want to talk to you."

"What about?"

"Do you really love Brad?"

The girl was suspicious. "Yes."

"Do you want to marry him?"

"No." Then the floodgates burst. "We're gonna run away. We're going to move to Vancouver, and never see any of you people again. I hate you. Can't you get it into your skull that I really hate you?"

"I've got an idea," Stephanie said. "You get Brad over and I'll give you enough money so that you can move to Vancouver."

Brad was suspicious, but he came over. Stephanie gave them two thousand dollars she had taken from her account, and she helped Greta pack. She knew that what she was doing was wicked, but she couldn't help herself. In fact, Greta was full of affection as they kissed good-bye and she got on the motorcycle and headed out to Vancouver. More like a daughter than she had ever been.

Then she took Hans out to a downtown bar, and told him she'd buy him anything he wanted to drink. The bartender was suspicious, but Stephanie told him that her son was certainly old enough to drink, and so he served them. Hans couldn't believe his luck. He ordered whiskey sours and martinis and manhattans and three zombies in a row. Then Stephanie drove him around until they came to a doughnut shop with a patrol car parked in the lot. She parked as close to the patrol car as she could. Then she got out and handed Hans the keys. She told him to back out and drive the car around to the front. Then she went around the doughnut shop and got on a bus. She heard the crunch through the bus window and saw the policemen running out to their car. Then she went home.

A few days later, the anchorman returned from Nagorno-Karabach.

"Hi honey, I'm home."

"Good. I missed you."

"So did I. Where are the kids?"

"Gone."

"What do you mean gone?"

"They're gone away. Now there's just you and me. And we can live happily ever after."

But the anchorman was not at all sympathetic. When he discovered that his daughter had run off to Vancouver with a motorcyclist and that his son was in jail, he was even less sympathetic. He ordered Stephanie out of his house and immediately filed for divorce. Then he flew to Vancouver and brought his daughter back and he hired a good lawyer and got his son out of jail. He convinced his first wife that they should get back together for the sake of the children, and they did. Hans kept getting drunk and stealing cars and Greta kept running away to live with increasingly more decadent bikers. They spent the rest of their days in misery.

As for Stephanie, she went back to the famous Canadian poet. He had to wash more now, because he had a job as writer-in-residence at a university, and he still didn't have any children. Stephanie kept her toothbrush in her purse so that nobody else could use it. When they merged the magazine she worked for with the other magazine, they made Stephanie the design editor for both publications, and gave her a small raise. She lived happily ever after, except for the times when she was in the company of children, and she kept that to a minimum.

THE WAITRESS

he waitress wakes in the grey, hurt dawn. She smells smoke on her clothes, grease on her skin. She has punched her pillow into a tight ball. K.T. Oslin is singing on the clock radio, a song about damaged love. The waitress wouldn't mind damaged love. She would welcome a heartache, because that would mean that for at least a little while someone would have loved her.

She has been reading the advertisements in *Vanity Fair* magazine. She doesn't read the articles. They have nothing to do with her. She doesn't really care about the clothes and perfumes that are being advertised. She cares only about the gestures, the way the models hold their bodies, extend their arms or legs, raise their chins, whirl their hair. She realizes that it is not the clothes that make them beautiful. If that were the case she could never enter that world. But often the clothes are ugly, and the models are nevertheless beautiful. That is the trick she wants to learn.

In the shower, she thinks about love. Her mother does not love her, nor does her stepfather. The men who touch her body as they offer her a tip do not love her. She knows some young, decent men who would fall in love with her if she would let them. But they are all married, and they are all poor. Some of them are good. They are fine and decent and would treat her well. But she does not want to be treated well. She does not want to mother children and be given small gifts on mother's day. She does not want to wash the dishes with the other women after the men have barbecued the steaks and are drinking beer out by the garage.

She wants someone who will love her for her gestures, someone who will not even see her behind the gestures. She doesn't mind getting hurt, or doesn't think she will mind, though you can never know for sure. She remembers a Joni Mitchell song with a line about a mean old daddy. That's what she wants. A mean old daddy who will love her and take her to Paris and buy her diamonds, and if he abandons her in Rome or in Athens, she will be ready for it.

She looks in the mirror. She has the body of a model, too thin and too tall. She was afraid for a while that her breasts were too large, but a shift in fashion favours her. Her jaw is angular, her cheekbones high. She knows she is awkward, but she thinks she can use this. Awkward gestures are more powerful than fluid ones. It all depends on the timing.

She looks at herself in the mirror. She prefers her mirror self, a clean surface extended over a smooth plane. She likes the way that mirrors can distort the body, stretching it thin. The polished bodies of cars release a shorter, fatter self. She would like to see herself in a prism, multiplied. She remembers when, as a child, she was a figure skater. This is the only memory she has that satisfies her. She worked very hard at the figures, and though other girls were better at free-style skating, she could inscribe perfect figure eights in the ice, and that was enough to make her happy.

Her skin is the problem. She wants to be free of imperfections, but that is difficult for a waitress. The work is hard, she is often hungry, and the food is greasy. She has tried to live on vegetables, but they will not sustain her through a fourteen-hour shift. Every time she nears perfection, her body betrays her.

She has nearly given up sex. She sometimes goes to movies or dances with Larry, who is left-handed and stutters, who also thinks about getting the gestures right. She does not have sex with Larry, who has never requested it anyway. Sometimes she picks up a man at a singles bar and goes to bed with him, but it is never satisfactory. He believes in profit, or he believes in God. He believes in something, and the waitress finds it hard to listen. The next day she feels violated, as if someone has broken into her home and stolen something she values.

And of course it happens. As soon as she gets it right, the waitress is beautiful, in any way that matters. But there is no point in being loved by truck drivers and construction workers, people who want barbecues and children. And there is no more point in being loved by lawyers who want only more expensive barbecues, or doctors, who want only more demanding children.

The waitress needs an artist or a politician. She needs somebody unencumbered by the real world. A professor would do. Somebody who believes in ideas. Somebody who doesn't care if it works. It would be nice, she thinks, to look over a northern lake, frozen, or an African plain, tattered with the remains of imaginary animals.

She wonders whether, if she were draped over the shoulder of a naked man for an advertisement in *Vanity Fair,* she could achieve the deadness of flesh they would need. She knows she could whirl her hair so that it would obscure her face. She needs only that small confusion that lasts for a second. She could handle that. She could make love to men who were mean and selfish and only wanted to use her. That would be fair. She would not have to give them anything. Their bodies would be smooth and silken, and they would be gone without apology. That's not so bad.

And, of course, one day it happens. The waitress is dancing in a dark bar with someone, and later, when she returns to her drink, a man in a suit gives her a business card. Call him or not, he says. It's only business. He doesn't buy her a drink, and a few minutes later he is gone. The next day she calls him, and before long she is a model, nothing big, but she appears on the back page of the second section of the newspaper in a business suit wearing a pair of glasses. She cuts out the ad and frames it and hangs it on her wall. She quits her job as a waitress, and in a few days she no longer smells of cigarette smoke and grease.

Suddenly there is money. She travels on airlines. Around her are men who give curt orders. She works very hard, as hard as when she was a waitress. But now she is a model, and she is taught how to walk, and somebody fixes her teeth. Nobody takes advantage of her. Nobody asks her to sleep with him. She still studies the ads in magazines until one day she imitates a gesture of a model in an ad for hair spray and realizes she is imitating herself. Then later she can no longer pick herself out in ads.

She senses that she is invisible. Clerks take no notice of her in stores until she insists they do. Then they are embarrassed. At parties, nobody comes to talk to her. She feels as if she is stretched tightly across the surface of her life, so thin that she reflects light. She reads articles about finding your true self. What might that be, she wonders, your true self.

And she grows older. There is nothing she can do about that. She doesn't fear the future. The other models are planning to retire soon, in a year or two, and become actresses when their bodies fail. But the waitress who is now a model doesn't worry about that. It is not her body that they want, only her gestures, and if she grows older, then she will learn new gestures, the gestures of the old.

What she misses is desire. She sees herself as without depth. There is no absence in her, no gap to be filled. She plays Gorecki's *Symphony of Sorrows* as she goes to sleep. The next morning she plays K.T. Oslin. She prefers K.T. Oslin. She goes to Australia to model dresses in the outback. When she returns, she is interviewed by a newspaper. The reporter asks her what she liked best about Australia. She thinks for a while. The cornflakes, she tells him. They have really good cornflakes.

At some point her stepfather is arrested for molesting young girls. Everyone assumes she has been abused as a child, but that is wrong. Her stepfather, though he does not love her, is a perfect gentleman. She cannot imagine him molesting anyone, and when he is freed, even though it is only on a technicality, she is glad. She buys a dog.

The dog is a mistake, even though he is an Afghan hound, just the right dog for a model. He introduces disorder into her life. He shits on the floor, and after she has cleaned it up, the smell of disinfectant lingers for weeks. He loves her madly. He licks her, nuzzles her, snuffles his nose against her without shame. When she is angry with him he whines and abases himself. He rolls sad eyes at her. When she forgives him he is delirious with joy and breaks the ornaments. She thinks about the dog at work, wonders whether he is happy, and she is angry with herself. He is only a dog. Then he is run over before her eyes, and she weeps for weeks. She does not buy another dog.

And her mother dies. It's impossible, she thinks, she is much too young to die, a mother who is only fifty-one. Cancer, they tell her, some problem in the reproductive system, something with a Latin name. They should have called her, but her mother wouldn't let them. Leave the girl be, her mother said. She's got problems of her own.

Maybe I am being tested, the model thinks. She tries to remember the story of Job, but she doesn't know the Bible, and she can't find the passage she wants. Besides, she doesn't believe in God. She imagines the universe as one of those glass balls that make it snow when you turn them upside down.

She dresses in black, and every Sunday she places a rose on her mother's grave. Sometimes she thinks that there is something she should have said to her mother when her mother was alive, but she can't imagine what it might be. Her mother is easier to talk to dead, and her daughter comes to love her.

Then a photographer takes a picture of her dressed in black, in an October dawn at her mother's grave. There is even fog. He shoots with a telephoto lens at a fair distance, and the picture is everywhere. It is a perfect picture, all the gestures of grief, but after it is published the model can no longer visit the grave of her mother. There is nobody there she can talk to.

The model has trouble understanding money. She knows exactly what you can do with a waitress's salary, but anything larger bewilders her. She checks her bank account like she checks the oil in her car. If there is money in the account, she spends it. If not, she waits until the account fills itself up again, and then she spends it. She has investments, but somebody else takes care of them. She sends a charitable donation to the university she would have gone to if she'd had enough money. After that they send her letters every week, so she doesn't give them any more in the hope that they will stop writing to her.

Nothing happens. The model reads about herself in magazine articles, but nothing they tell her is true. She goes to exotic places. Calcutta, Odessa, Reykjavik. Nothing happens. She parachutes from airplanes. She dives in shark-infested waters. She always comes back to the same place.

Finally she takes to waiting. She waits in airports, she waits in bus depots and train stations. She waits in malls and in theatres. She goes to restaurants and watches the women who serve. They are ordinary people doing a job. She waits by her window when the rain falls steadily in May, and she waits while the first snow falls in November. She is waiting still.

Samantha, The Shampoo, & The Sheik

ne day, not so very long ago, a beautiful daughter was born to a poor but honest trucker and his wife. They named her Samantha, because both the trucker and his wife were fans of a television program named *Bewitched*. They planned to have a second daughter and name her Tabitha, but no second daughter came along.

Samantha grew to be a beautiful young woman who hated her name, because everyone called her Sam. She even got mail addressed to her as Mr. Sam Buckle. At the same time, because her parents also made her watch reruns of *Bewitched,* she developed a strong sense of personal destiny and belief in the possibilities of magic in the world.

So it was no surprise to Samantha when she won the Morden Apple Queen contest, and when she stood first in her hairdressing class at the Fillmont School of Commercial Success, she knew it was her due. Still, after a year working long hours at the Hair Apparent Beauty Salon, she decided to go and seek her fortune.

"I'm going to Hollywood to seek my fortune," she told her

parents one day in June. "I have saved my salary for several months, and I wish to become the hairdresser to the stars."

Of course, her parents tried to talk her out of her plan. Her father listened to the radio on his long trucking hauls across the continent, and he was wise in the ways of the world.

"Don't do it Honey," he said. "Those Hollywood types are wolves. They'll eat you alive."

"Why don't you stay home and marry Randy," her mother said. "He's got a good job at the flour mill, and he hardly drinks at all. And you know he's in love with you."

Samantha was adamant. "Randy's a nice boy," she said. "But he'll have to marry one of the other hairdressers. I have my dreams, and I'm going to make them come true."

And of course her parents couldn't argue with that. They had always told her to follow her dreams, only they had expected her to dream about a nice house and three lovely children.

It was a very long bus ride all the way from Morden to Hollywood, and Samantha was tired when she got there. She was hardly a half block from the hotel when a nice young man offered her a job in a massage parlour at a very high salary, and offered to train her for free. Samantha refused. Even though the job seemed attractive, her dream was to be the most famous hairdresser in the entire world, and she did not want to get sidetracked from her dream the first day in Hollywood.

It was hard at first, but Samantha had expected it to be hard, and she wasn't a quitter. All the streets of Hollywood were lined with hairdressing salons, but none of them needed another hairdresser.

Then one day, when she was just about out of money, she got her chance. She was just dropping off her resume at Hair Today, Gone Tomorrow, when one of the hairdressers quit in a rage.

"I don't have to put up with this," the young woman shouted. "I trained as a hairdresser, not as a make-up artist for a freak show." And she stomped out of the salon.

94

The manager glanced at Samantha's application.

"You want a job?" he said. "There's your first customer." And he nodded at a woman who was sitting in a chair near the door. She was the ugliest woman that Samantha had ever seen. She was dressed in rags, and her hair was so dirty it was impossible to know what colour it was. She was covered with warts.

Samantha drew a deep breath. "Right," she said. "Welcome to Hair Today, Gone Tomorrow. What can I do for you?"

"Just make me beautiful," the old crone cackled, and she slid into the chair in front of Samantha. She smelled terrible, but Samantha just wiggled her nose in the way she had, and she set to work. First, she washed the hair, which turned out to be blonde. The ends were all split, so Samantha cut the ends and styled in the very style she had used to come first in class at the Fillmont School of Success. The hair was quite long, and the more Samantha combed it, the more beautiful it became. The old woman now seemed very strange, because her hair was undeniably beautiful, though she still looked like a witch.

"Would you like the full beauty treatment?" Samantha asked the old woman.

"Yes, indeed," she cackled. "The full beauty treatment. Yes, indeed." Samantha began with the manicure. As she worked on the old, arthritic hands, they began to look young and lovely. Then she did a facial, laying on unguents and lotions and covering the face with hot towels. By now the manager and the other hairdressers had gathered around. They began by laughing at the beautiful hair and hands on the old woman, but when Samantha removed the towels and wiped the old woman's face they gasped. There was the most beautiful face they had ever seen. The warts and wrinkles were all gone. The old woman, who was now revealed as a beautiful young woman, waved the others away, and took Samantha aside.

"Seventy years ago I was a famous movie star," the woman told her. "Then an evil film director cast a spell upon me because I refused to marry him. I have had to wander the world until my beauty could be restored by someone who would offer me complete generosity. You are that person, and if you ever need anything, just call on me." And she gave Samantha her card. It said "Mary Pickford" and it gave an address in Beverly Hills. She also paid for the beauty treatment and left a seventy-five dollar tip.

The manager, however, was not impressed. He thought that Samantha had played some trick, and he told her not to bother coming back the next day.

Poor Samantha wandered the streets of Hollywood for another week. Her seventy-five dollars was almost gone when she found a shop in a poor and rundown section of Beverly Hills. The shop was called Scissor's Palace, and the manager was a hefty but good-humoured woman.

"Choose one of the customers and show me what you can do," the manager said. Samantha looked over the group. All of them seemed like ordinary upper-middle class women with blue hair, but one stood out. She was terribly thin and stringy, very old and wrinkled, and her long greasy blonde hair hung down nearly to her waist.

Samantha took her to a chair and sat her down. The old woman smelled very bad, but Samantha just twitched her nose in the way she had and asked, "The whole beauty treatment?" The woman nodded, and Samantha began. She washed the hair, cut out the split ends, styled it and brushed it until it shone so that it lit up the room. Then she manicured the hands until they looked like a young woman's. And of course, when she had finished the facial, the face that looked back at her was hauntingly beautiful.

"Thank you," the woman told her. "You have saved me from a fate worse than death. An evil evangelist cast a spell on me because I would not do his bidding, and I have had to wander the world until I found someone who was perfectly generous. You are that person, and because you have been so good to me, feel free to call on me if you ever need anything." And she gave Samantha her card. It said "Aimee Semple Macpherson" and it gave an address. She paid her bill and gave Samantha a seventy-five dollar tip.

The manager said, "That was very impressive. But it seemed a little strange. I can't take any chances with the supernatural. The cops around here are really hard on magic. Sorry. You really are good, but take my advice and go back to Canada where nobody will notice."

Samantha did not take her advice, but it did give her an idea. The next day she took a bus to Palm Springs, then made her way to Rancho Mirage. She went to a unisex beauty salon called Hair Canada, and they gave her a job immediately. Her first customer was an old man with dirty fingernails, long unkempt black hair and ugly sores on his face. Samantha didn't hesitate a second. She washed and trimmed his hair and brushed it until it gleamed. Then she manicured his hands, and watched the health and boyish strength return to them. When she removed the towels after the facial, she looked into the most handsome face she had ever seen.

"How can I ever thank you?" the man said. "A spell was cast on me by an evil producer because I would not procure starlets for him, and I have had to wander the world like this for nearly seventy years. Only your perfect goodness was able to save me."

Then he gave her his card that read "Rudolph Valentino", he paid for his treatment, and he left her a seventy-five dollar tip.

The manager at Hair Canada wanted Samantha to stay on, but she quit the next morning. She went back to Hollywood and called on Mary Pickford. Mary was happy to see Samantha. She had just signed a seven-year contract with Warner Brothers under another name, and she was looking for a personal beautician. They agreed to terms, and Samantha went on to visit Aimee Semple Macpherson. She had just signed on as a Televangelist with a famous church, under a pseudonym, of course, and she too needed a personal beautician. It took only a few minutes for them to come to terms.

Then she went to visit Rudolph. He had just signed a contract to do a remake of a film about dinosaurs under a pseudonym, but he didn't need a personal beautician. Instead, he asked Samantha to marry him. Of course, she agreed.

Then just before her wedding, her parents came to Hollywood to beg her to come back to Morden in time for the Apple Festival. Randy came too, and begged her to give up her glitzy life and come back to Morden and marry him. Samantha gave each of her parents a handful of money, and she gave Randy a long slow kiss so that he would know what he'd missed. Then she and Rudy got into the Ferrari and drove off into the California hills.

RETURN OF THE FROGS

 nce, in a slightly better time than our own, a farmer lived with his wife and daughter on a farm just outside Portage la Prairie. His daughter was neither very beautiful nor very good, but she was the only daughter he had and he loved her dearly. Her name was Virginia, but she had rechristened herself Gina.

Gina was fifteen and she planned to be an NHL goalie when she grew up. She was already the top goalie in the midget B league in the Southwest Manitoba Amateur Hockey League, and only six months ago, in an exhibition game against Fargo, North Dakota, she'd had a shutout.

One day she was throwing her baseball against the side of the barn when it bounced crazily and fell into an old well. She looked into the well, but instead of seeing her ball, she saw a frog.

"Hey you!" she shouted to the frog who was swimming around in the water. "How about getting my ball out of the well?"

The frog made a noise that sounded like "chuggarumm."

"No, I'm serious," she said. "If you get my ball out of that well, you can eat off my plate and sleep in my bed and everything. And if you're really good, I'll give you a kiss and turn you into a fairy prince. Then we can get married and live happily ever after."

The frog didn't reply, but he dived down into the well and disappeared. Gina waited a few minutes, but no frog appeared so she walked back to the house. The school bus would be by in a few minutes anyway.

"You're not going to school dressed like that," her mother told her. "Put on something decent, and make it snappy. The bus will be here in a minute."

"What's wrong with what I'm wearing?" Gina asked.

"You'll be mistaken for the janitor," her mother replied. "And if I'm not mistaken, there's manure on the cuffs of those jeans. Now change."

"Sheesh."

"And don't swear. It's not becoming in a lady."

"I didn't swear. I just said sheesh. And I'm not a lady. The only ladies in this place are members of the Ladies Aid, and you can't join until you're ninety."

"You are getting entirely too big for your britches, young lady. I swear, I don't know what I'm going to do with you."

"You shouldn't swear," Gina told her, skipping out of the room. "It isn't nice."

She missed the bus of course. She put on a miniskirt, and her mother wouldn't let her wear that either. Finally she dressed in a pair of slacks and a sweater that made her look like a bag of potatoes, but her mother thought she looked nice.

"She's missed the bus again, Roy," her mother said. "I don't know how she's going to survive in the world by herself. Can you give her a lift to school?"

"Sure," her dad said. "I got to go to town to get a carburetor kit for the John Deere anyway. C'mon, Princess."

Gina's dad let her drive the half-ton all the way to the edge of the town. Then he dropped her off at the new high school. The bell had rung, but most of the kids were still outside. "Be good," her dad said. "Don't take any wooden nickles."

"You're a sweetheart, Roy," Gina said, and she blew him a kiss. She'd started calling him Roy a couple of months ago, but not when her mother was around. He seemed to like it, but it enraged her mother. She'd once called her Margaret instead of Mom and been grounded for a week.

School had just started a couple of weeks ago, and nothing was settled yet. Last year, her best friend had been Trish, but now Trish was best friends with Cristal, and Gina didn't think it was fair. The town kids could play together all summer, but she had to help on the farm, so when she got back to school every fall things were all changed.

Math class was the last class of the day, and Miss Miller, who taught it, was Gina's favourite teacher. She caught Gina after class and asked if she could have a few words with her.

"As long as I catch my bus," Gina said. "I missed it this morning, and if I miss it again I'm in deep doo-doo."

"It'll just take a minute. Look, Gina, we're having try-outs for cheerleaders on Wednesday. If you want to come out, I'll give you a ride home afterward. You're really athletic, and I think you'd have a really good chance. Both Trish and Cristal are trying out."

"No," Gina said. "No thanks. I'd sooner be the one who gets cheered."

"Are you going out for hockey again?"

"You bet."

"Look, Gina," her teacher said. "I'm all for liberation and equal opportunities. You know that. But are you sure that playing hockey is a realistic choice? It keeps you kind of isolated from the rest of the kids."

"That's their problem," Gina said. "I've got to catch a bus. So long."

When Gina got home, her baseball was drying out on the front steps.

"I scooped it out for you with the fish net," her dad said. "It should be okay as soon as it dries out."

"Thanks, Roy. You didn't happen to see a frog, did you?"

101

"As a matter of fact, I did. Great big bugger. He must have fallen in. I scooped him out too and let him go."

"He's actually an enchanted prince," Gina told her father. "I told him that if I got my ball back he could eat off my plate and sleep in my bed. I suppose he'll be around later."

"Don't you go kissing any frogs," her dad said. "Not when you're fifteen. I've got enough problems around here. Finish university, then you can kiss all the frogs you want."

"I'm not going to university," she reminded him. "I'm going to be an NHL goalie."

"Right," he said. "I forgot. Anyway, I've got cows to milk, Princess. You go on in and study. And try not to fight with your mom."

"Are you sure she's my mom? Mightn't she actually be a wicked stepmother?"

"She's your mom, all right. Forty-eight hours of labour and she still hasn't forgotten it. Be good, please?"

"Right on, Roy. You go round up the herd, and I'll deal with Dale Evans."

Gina's mother was in the kitchen making jelly. The kitchen was full of steam and her mother's glasses were covered with steam from the boiling jelly.

"Anything I can get you?" Gina asked. "Eye of newt or tail of frog? Finger of birth-strangled dog?"

"If you're going to quote Shakespeare," her mother said, "try to get it right." Her mother had been an English teacher in some distant, unthinkable past, and she seemed to have memorized every poem in the English language. At the moment, she looked exasperated.

"Whatever," Gina answered, and she brooded for a minute on a fly that was circling the butter dish. "I was talking to Miss Miller today," she went on. "She wants me to go out for cheerleaders."

"And?" said her mother, leaving the question hanging there.

"I think maybe I will."

"I don't think you'd like it much," her mother said. "You're not the type."

"What is that supposed to mean?" Gina asked. "Not the pretty type? Not the sexy type?"

"Not the cheerleader type," her mother said. "And you know precisely what I mean."

"Too cranky, too bad-tempered, too hard to get along with?"

"Precisely."

And Gina did not go out for cheerleaders, because she suspected that her mother was right. She did go out for the juvenile hockey team. There was a new coach this year, a guy named Semchuk, who had played in the AHL and had been called up for one game with the Red Wings but had been thrown out of the game in the first period for fighting. He was good-looking in a barnyard sort of way, but very bad tempered. He didn't even want Gina to try out, because he said he was looking for the league title and he didn't want to wreck the team's chances. Still, he let her come to the first couple of practices and even grudgingly admitted that she was pretty good for a girl. But when he posted the roster her name was not on it. Instead, Danny Reimer was the first goalie, and the back-up was Bill Klassen, who couldn't even skate.

Gina was weeping in a back stall in the barn when her father found her.

"Hey, Princess," he said. "NHL goalies don't cry."

"It's not fair," Gina told him. "I'm better than anybody else that tried out. I'm the only chance we've got to win the league title. But I'm not going to get a chance." And she started to cry again.

"Hold on. Hold on," her father said. "It's not the end of the world."

"Yes it is," Gina said. "It is the end of the world. It's the end of my world. It's the end of everything I ever wanted."

But the world didn't end. Gina went out for cheerleaders, and, as Miss Miller had predicted, she made it. And, as her mother had predicted, she hated every minute of it. She hated the other girls, and they hated her because she was the only one who got every drill perfect. And she hated the uniform. And she detested football because it was a stupid game.

"There's a frog in the basement," her mother told her. "A huge horrible green frog. Can you get rid of it?"

"Right," Gina said. "Exactly what I need."

"What are you doing here?" Gina asked the frog when she found it behind the dryer in the basement. "You didn't come through. No free wishes for this girl."

The frog made a croaking noise, possibly "chugarumm," and he jumped into the corner where her baseball and glove were lying.

"Oh," Gina said. "The ball. But you didn't get it. Roy did. He had to rescue you as well."

The frog didn't say anything. He just puffed out his cheeks.

"All right," Gina told it. "A bargain's a bargain." And she took the frog up to her room and put it in a cage that had been empty since her hamster, Jeffrey, had died a couple of years ago. Then she went around the house catching flies for it. There weren't very many, but she found some dead ones between the windows in her room and gave them to him. That night, just as she was going to bed, she picked up the frog. He was sort of dried out, and not slimy at all. She held him up to the light.

"Now if I give you a kiss," she said, "you have to promise to turn into a prince." The frog blinked its big eyes. "Here goes," and she planted a big, noisy kiss on the top of his head. Nothing happened.

"Right," Gina said. "A dud. A misfire. A blank cartridge. With my luck you'll turn out to have some disgusting disease and I'll catch it and die."

The next day, the frog was gone. Vanished. No amount of searching could find him. But there was a new guy in school, and all the girls were buzzing about him. His name was Jean-Claude Grenwill, and his father was the new dentist in town. Within a week, he was the first-string quarterback, and the team, which hadn't won a game until then, finally had need for cheerleaders.

Gina went out for a Coke with Trish and Cristal and tried as hard as she could not to get into a fight with either of them.

They reported the rumour that Jean-Claude had a girlfriend back in Montreal who was an actress and that none of the local girls was going to have a chance.

And yet, only a couple of weeks later, Jean-Claude hung around after the football practice watching the cheerleaders do their drills. Gina was intensely conscious of her body and her little uniform. She wished she could put on her goalie uniform, complete with mask. After the drills, Jean-Claude came up to her.

"You're really good," he told her. "You're a terrific athlete."

"This is my last practice," she said. "I'm turning in my uniform. No more cheerleading for me."

"That's too bad," Jean-Claude said. "This team needs all the cheering it can get."

"I don't want to cheer," Gina said. "I want to play." It seemed important to her that she make him understand that she wasn't really a cheerleader.

"You want to play football?"

"No. Hockey. I'm a goalie. I'm the best goalie in the whole goddam province and they won't let me play." And she burst into tears.

"Whoa, wait," he said. "What's this all about?"

And so she told him everything. She told him how rotten and corrupt the world was, and how unfair everything was, and she ended by telling him that if he wanted to watch her boobs bounce in a skimpy uniform, he could forget about that too. And, as a postscript, she mentioned that she hated him.

"Hang on," he said. "I've got an idea." And he told her about a special hockey school that was being held in Montreal at Christmas, just for goalies. And he told her that it was being run by the most famous NHL goalie who had ever lived, a name that took her breath away.

"Great," she said. "It will only cost a billion dollars, and they won't let me in because I'm a girl."

But she talked to Roy, and Roy talked to Margaret, and in the end it turned out that they had some money they had been saving for a trip to Hawaii, but they had decided not to go to

Hawaii after all. There was enough money to send her to Montreal, and so she went. The famous goalie made her work harder than she had ever worked in her life, and he made her forget all the tricks she had ever learned and just concentrate on stopping the puck.

Then Danny Reimer got sick over Christmas and Bill Klassen broke his leg skiing, so the coach phoned her and asked if she'd fill in for a game. She did, and she got a shutout, and Jean-Claude sat behind the goal and cheered like crazy.

After the game Jean-Claude walked her over to the Mitchell's place where her parents were waiting for her to drive her back to the farm. Just before they got to the door, they stopped, and Jean-Claude kissed her, a long, lovely kiss.

Gina stepped back. "Please don't be offended," she told him, "but you look an awful lot like a frog I used to know."

HEART'S DESIRE

n a certain town in southern Saskatchewan, on a January night, a man named Karl Anderson had just celebrated his thirty-sixth birthday. That day, he'd received a particularly nasty card from his ex-wife, he'd quarrelled with his boss and been fired, and he'd drunk thirteen bottles of beer. He stumbled on the sidewalk just outside the bar, and an icy hand reached out and squeezed his heart.

The last thing he remembered was falling into the snow and thinking how unfair it was to die at the age of thirty-six. When he woke up in the hospital, the doctor told him his heart was severely damaged. He was going to need a heart transplant.

He remembered reading newspaper articles about the long wait for hearts, and he was pretty sure he would die before his turn came. But a couple of weeks later, they rushed him to London, Ontario. For a few weeks his life was defined by tubes and needles and glowing red dials. He hovered on the edge of an abyss, and he would have chosen death if he could have. But a few weeks later he was home with a new heart.

"Good as new," the doctor told him. "You're a lucky man. You've got a second chance. Don't muck up your life this time."

Karl objected, but he lived in a small town, and there was no sense denying the facts. The doctor knew him as well as anyone: his drinking, his fights, his record of failure. He had messed up his life. He resolved to do better.

But strange things started to happen to him. He developed a liking for pickled beets, and he had never eaten them in his life. He found he could carry a tune, though he had always regarded himself as singularly unmusical. He was developing powerful muscles in his shoulders and forearms. And the second time he woke up in the night shouting, he went back to see his doctor.

"It's crazy," he told the doctor. "It's as if I got more than just a new heart. I seem to have got a bunch of new feelings as well."

"That's not an uncommon fantasy," the doctor told him. "Often after a heart transplant, the recipient feels guilty that he's still alive and the donor is dead. Sometimes people do stupid things. Try to ignore it and get on with your life."

But Karl couldn't ignore it. He was now afraid of dogs. He'd started taking cream and sugar in his coffee. He preferred wine to beer. And his heart had started to talk to him at night.

"We've got to get back," it told him one night. "It's nearly winter. Debby and the kids are counting on me."

"Where?" he asked the heart, sitting up in bed. "Where do we have to go?" But the heart just thumped in his chest and refused to answer.

"The family requested anonymity," the doctor told him. "When they called me from London, all they said was that the heart came from a thirty-six year old man of about your size and weight."

"Where did he live?" Karl asked the doctor.

"I don't know. Somewhere in southern Ontario, I guess. He was killed in a motorcycle accident."

The next day, Karl drove to Regina. He went to the public library and began to look up all the southern Ontario newspapers from the day before his heart transplant. There was no report of a thirty-six-year-old man killed in a motorcycle accident. Karl went home and brooded.

The heart became more insistent. "The crop will be ready," it told him. "All those apples to harvest, and Debby all alone. We've got to get home."

Karl found that he could swim. And he seemed to remember skiing, though he had never skied. He had to take a larger size in shoes.

Finally, he went back to the library in Regina. He got a map of southern Ontario that showed all the apple-growing areas. Then he got all the obituaries from all the local papers and looked for thirty-six-year-old men. After a week of searching, he found what he was after. The obituary was in the local paper from Niagara-on-the-Lake. Carl Peters, aged thirty-six, survived by his wife Debby and daughters Linda and Ashley. The cause of death was not mentioned.

Karl took his secret knowledge back with him. There was no reason to believe he had actually made a discovery. Ontario was a large province. Dozens of thirty-six-year-old men died every day. Some of them would have wives named Debby. Meanwhile, he had forgotten his ex-wife's name. When he tried to think of his childhood, he could recall only dim figures: a mother, a father, perhaps a brother or a sister, he couldn't be sure.

When he told his doctor he was going to Niagara-on-the-Lake, the doctor sent him to a psychiatrist. To his surprise, the psychiatrist was sympathetic.

"It's something you're going to have to get out of your system," she told him. "Go there and look around, but don't try to contact the family. That would be harassment. I think you'll find that nothing is really familiar and you'll recognize that your obsession has no basis in fact."

Karl took all his savings from the bank and bought travellers' cheques. The heart was quiet once it knew that they were going and that a ticket had been bought.

"We're going next week," he told it at night, but it only

pulsed regularly. Karl seemed to be able to take enormous breaths, to fill his lungs with gallons of air.

The trip to Toronto was uneventful, but after they'd landed and got on the bus for Niagara-on-the-Lake, the heart seemed to speed up, and Karl started to feel anxious. The freeways of Toronto and the grey apartment blocks of Mississauga seemed strange and foreign to Karl, who had never been east of Winnipeg. But once they were out of the concrete and into apple-orchard country, everything began to seem familiar. He noted with approval the orderly ranks of tree on tree, heavy with the fall harvest.

When he got to Niagara-on-the-Lake, Karl rented a motel room and a car. Then he looked up Carl Peters in the telephone book. For a moment he panicked when he couldn't find the number, then he realized that Carl's wife would have put the telephone in her own name. He found the address and called. A female voice said "Hello, hello, hello?" Karl hung up the phone.

That night in the bed in the motel room, the heart was insistent. "I've got to get out there and pick those apples," it said. "There's no time to sleep." And it woke him several times during the night, calling out Debby's name.

The next morning, Karl stopped at a garage on the outskirts of town. He asked if anyone could tell him the way to Carl Peters's farm. The young man at the counter had never heard of him, but he called an old mechanic out from the back, and the old mechanic said, "Carl Peters is dead. Got himself killed just after New Year's. Nicest guy you ever met, but a stubborn fool for that damn motorcycle. Didn't leave a lick of insurance." And he told Karl the farm was three miles south, right on the same road he was travelling.

Karl drove out to the farm. A sign right at the driveway read Carl Peters, Apple Country Orchards. At least that hadn't been changed. A couple of small dogs barked at his wheels when he turned around in the driveway, and a couple of little girls played in the yard to the side of the house. A face peeked out of window, and Karl backed out and drove away.

On the way back, he noticed that a motorcycle, a Harley-Davidson, was for sale at the very garage where he had stopped that morning. It was Carl Peters's bike, a bit scuffed from the accident but still running. Karl gave the mechanic four thousand dollars. The mechanic told him he could use dealer plates for a couple of days until he could get insurance.

"Debby's going to be real grateful for that money," the old mechanic told him. "Her husband didn't leave her nothing but a mountain of debt."

Driving the motorcycle was a dream. Karl found a country road, kicked it up to a hundred and twenty miles an hour. His heart sang inside him, and he felt more at peace than he had since the transplant.

The heart wouldn't let him sleep at all that night. He tossed in his motel bed, his mind filled with images of giant apples and motorcycles. The heart sang something insistent, but he couldn't make out the words.

The next morning he knocked at Debby's door. A thin, small woman with a pinched face opened the door. Karl was disappointed. He'd hoped she'd be beautiful. Still, he told her he was looking for work.

"Have you ever picked apples?" she asked.

"I used to run my own orchard," he told her. "But that was a long time ago."

"I need a man," she said. "My husband died this winter and I'm running this place myself. I couldn't afford one until yesterday when I sold his motorcycle." She looked over at the motorcycle Karl had parked in the driveway. Her eyes opened wide.

"Not a Harley-Davidson?" Karl asked.

She nodded. "Yes."

"What a coincidence."

He started working that very day. It was as if he had picked apples all his life. He collected bushel after bushel, never letting a single apple fall to earth. The little girls came to help him and he teased them and they giggled and ran, and peeked out at him from behind shrubs and from under baskets. He started so early and worked so late that it didn't make any sense for him to go to the motel in town. He made himself a bed in the corner of the toolshed, and he slept there. The heart was quiet now. It let him sleep all night.

Harvest turned into late fall, and late fall turned into winter. There was so much to do Karl didn't have a minute to spare. Debby thanked him for being so reliable, and wanted to pay him more than they had agreed, but he refused. Every so often, he would try to remember his life in Saskatchewan, but that seemed a very long time ago, and when he tried to remember details, they eluded him. Sometimes, Debby would bring him coffee out in the orchard where he was working, and always, after supper, before he went out to his bed in the toolshed, they would share a glass of sweet apple cider.

One night, Debby asked him to stay for a second glass. She had never talked about her husband before, but she did now. "He was the most dependable man in the world," she said. "As long as he was alive I didn't have to worry about anything." And she began to cry. Karl took her in his arms, and told her she'd never have to worry about anything again. Then she took him by the hand and led him into the bedroom.

That night Karl awoke in terrible pain. He knew that his heart had failed and that he was dying, but he wasn't afraid.

The next morning Carl Peters awoke at daybreak and got out of bed quietly so as not to awake Debby. He stretched languidly, and felt the strength in his new body. Somewhere, at the edge of his consciousness, the image of a wheat field shimmered, but he shook it off and hurried into the kitchen to make a pot of coffee. Outside, his orchard was waiting.

GIRL AND WOLF

t is morning. The possibilities for the wolf are open and endless. The paths through the forest run in every direction. The pale green new leaves on the trees are welcome after a hard winter. The breeze is gentle and ruffles his fur. The wolf is hungry, he is always hungry. That is what it is to be a wolf. The wolf is sleek and limber. As he runs, he admires his own grace.

The red-haired girl is going to see her grandmother. The weather is the same for her, same morning, same breeze, same new green leaves. The girl is tall and well made. She has already forgotten all her mother's cautions. She is ready to talk to strangers, she is eager for strangers and adventures. A girl's life is surrounded by cautions, she is circumscribed by rules. Only a forest offers freedom.

The paths through the forest run in all directions. They meet and intersect. They double back on themselves, intertwine. There are a thousand nodes, a thousand crossings. At any one of these crossings the girl might encounter the wolf. There are so many crossings that it is inevitable that at one of them the wolf and girl will meet.

When they meet, the wolf must ask the question, the girl must answer. Where are you going? To visit my grandmother. It is the question all the wolves ask, the answer all girls give. The girl's path is the path of needles, the wolf will follow the path of pins. Needles and pins, the path leads to the grandmother's house, all paths lead to the grandmother's house.

The wolf is there first. He is always first. He runs with his easy gait down the winding path. The girl is distracted. She strays from the path, she picks flowers, she stops to drink at a stream. The wolf is early. He must wait for the girl. It is only the start of his waiting. The wolf eats the grandmother. He must pass the time somehow, and he is hungry. Even then, and that takes some time, the grandmother is old and stringy, he must wait. He lies in the bed.

The girl knocks at the door. The wolf, in the bed, is nearly mad with impatience. He is sick with desire. "Come in," he shouts. The girl enters. The girl likes entrances. She is fresh and perfumed from the flowers she has picked. She dances in the door, her dress swirls, her red hair swirls. "Grandmother," she says, "see, I have picked you some flowers."

"Bring them here," the wolf answers. She gets a glass of water from the kitchen. She puts the flowers in the water and brings them to the bed. She knows that the wolf is not her grandmother. She recognizes him as the stranger she met in the forest. Still, she is calm. She seems to know what she is doing, or else she is caught by some force that makes her operate against her will.

"Come, get into the bed with me," the wolf tells the girl. It is a desperate ruse. If she recognizes him all will be lost. And how can she fail to recognize him? He is not even masked. All his life it has been like this. He is never properly prepared. He never has the disguise he needs, the mask he should wear.

"What shall I do with my coat?" she asks.

"Throw it in the fire," the wolf tells her. "You won't need it any more."

The girl takes off her coat and throws it into the fire. "And what shall I do with my dress?" she asks.

"Take it off and throw it into the fire. You won't need it any more."

She slips the dress over her head and throws it into the fire. She is wearing a white slip and red shoes. "What shall I do with my shoes?"

"Take them off and throw them into the fire. You won't be needing them any more."

The girl sits on the edge of the bed to take off her shoes. She bends with an awkwardness the wolf finds touching. She slips off one shoe at a time and throws them into the fire. "What shall I do with my slip?" she asks the wolf.

"Take it off and throw it into the fire. You won't be needing it any more." The girl pulls the slip over he head and throws it into the fire. She has on black panties and a black brassiere. Panties and brassiere are edged with lace. They look expensive.

"What shall I do with my brassiere?" the girl asks the wolf. Her red hair spills over the whiteness of her shoulders.

"Take it off and throw it into the fire. You won't be needing it any more." The wolf is tense. Is he perhaps too eager? He is trying to make his answers part of a ritual that will complete itself out of its inner necessity. One false step now and the charm might be broken.

The girl takes off her brassiere and throws it into the fire. Her breasts spill out, or at least the only words that come to the wolf's mind are "spill out." The girl's breasts are high and firm and very large. They accentuate the slimness of her waist. In the cool air of the room her nipples grow firm.

"And what shall I do with my panties?"

"Take them off and throw them into the fire. You won't need them any more."

The girl slips down her panties and flips them into the fire with her toe. She stands there, entirely naked. The little triangle is a paler red than her hair. The girl gets into the bed and snuggles up against the wolf. Her hair seems even redder against the white of the sheets.

"Why do you have so much hair on your body, Grandmother?" she asks. She rubs her hands along the wolf's body, and he feels rising in himself something that might have been hunger if he hadn't just eaten.

"It keeps me warm," the wolf replies.

"And why do you have such large eyes?" she asks, and as she asks, she looks at him with her own wide green eyes.

"The better to see you with," the wolf says, though he knows the inadequacy of that answer. He can feel her firm breasts pressed against his body.

"And why do you have such large teeth?" she asks. It is his moment. The wolf knows there will be no more questions. Everything depends on his answer now. He hesitates a moment, but there is really no option. There is only one answer, and there has never really been a choice. He says it reluctantly, "The better to eat you with."

"Nonsense," the girl replies, sliding under the wolf and pulling him on top of her. Her hands slip down to his hindquarters, easing his entry. The girl likes entrances. The wolf moans in his delight, a moan that blends with the ecstatic moans of all his ancestors. The girl is inexperienced but active, and when it is over, the wolf doesn't know whether what he feels is joy or pain.

The girl lights a cigarette from a package on her grandmother's table. She sits cross-legged on the bed, looking at the wolf. "That was nice," she says. "We're going to get along fine." She blows the smoke out her nostrils and flicks some ashes onto the floor. "It's a pity about my clothes, though. I'm going to have to get an entire new wardrobe. You don't have a job, I know that, but it will all work out. You can work at my dad's service station until something better comes along."

Just then there is a knock at the door. The girl finds a robe in her grandmother's closet. She slips it over her nakedness and goes to the door. A woodcutter stands there, his axe gleaming in his hand.

"Is everything all right?" he asks.

"Just fine," the girl says.

"I was wondering about your grandmother."

"Grandma's gone to Tucson, Arizona, to live with my aunt," the girl tells him. She's given the house to me and my fiancé. We're going to be doing some renovating, so if you're looking for work, why don't you drop around in a couple of weeks."

The wolf already knows the ending. It is the last of his wolfhood. His morning runs down the winding and criss-crossing trails of the forest are over. Already, his legs ache from the concrete on which he will stand. His fur is beginning to smell of oil. And so it has always been. What is the good of cautioning young girls? Grandmothers cannot be trusted. They are always somewhere else. The woodcutter is always too late. Whatever is lost is lost forever, and the forest trails, though they wind and cross, are searching for somebody else's meetings.

The Girl of
Milk & Blood

Giorgio

he cold dry bora is blowing again, down from the east beyond the mountains. My face is cracked, like the clay bottoms of the stream beds after the fall rains have run off into the valley below. Each crack is a tiny portion of agony, and the relentless wind fills them with dust. The women rub their faces with butter to keep them smooth, and that is good enough for a walk to the well, or over to the neighbour's place to gossip in the afternoon, but it is of no help for a day spent on the side of the mountain. The cattle are always thirsty, as if the dryness of the wind had sucked the very moisture from their bodies.

It is on days like this that I think of my boyhood further east in the underground caves and streams of the karst. Deep in the limestone caves, there was only one season, a cool dark season of crystal water and candlelight at noon. When I joined the brotherhood, I never dreamed of this godforsaken mountain with its impoverished valley below. I knew nothing of the disastrous rains that can wipe out a village in an hour, or the kind of stubborn people who would gather up their surviving relatives and rebuild their village in the path of the same murderous flood. I never thought of snow ten metres deep, or this devil of a drying wind.

There is beauty here, all right, but it is a spare, cramped beauty, the beauty of twisted dwarf juniper and green alder and stunted rhododendron. In the spring, the snowdrops peep out from the melting snow, and later there are gentian and saxifrage, rock jasmine, campion and primrose. If your eyes are keen, you might see rabbits or partridges or grouse and, once in a very long time, a golden eagle or a mountain roe. For the rest, you must satisfy yourself with vipers, salamanders and newts. And this is fitting, I suppose, because this is a community without forgiveness. Here, no wrong is ever forgotten, no insult ever properly redressed, even by death. Revenge seeps up from the valley below like a poisonous fog, and it dries our souls as surely as the bora dries our skin.

Bellemondo is the name of our village, a name left over from some hopeful past, though it is nothing but an irony now. Our sister villages are Pontebba and Comegliano, but no one ever goes to them. Once in a while some enterprising villager will take the mountain roads down to Udine and catch the train to Trieste, perhaps to buy a wedding dress for a daughter or to present a government official with some bewildering request. In this village we speak Friulan, and in the valley below the farmers speak Slovene. Italian is a foreign language, spoken only by the odd official who blunders into our village, and by our mayor, who is mayor only because he can speak Italian. We of the brotherhood speak it, of course, but we are considered outsiders, though all seven of us have spent most of our lives here. In this village you can be an outsider for generations.

Our village sits at the foot of an old castle, where once a baron ruled in feudal splendour, though there has been no baron here for over a century. Now, the castle belongs to the Americans, who repaired the high walls that surround it, and who, for a couple of weeks each summer, arrive in their four-wheel-drive vehicles and disappear behind the wall. They bring everything they need, so that they never have to speak to a villager. Or they used to. Now the Germans have taken over, though they are almost as distant as the Americans. Every few days a military vehicle drives through the town and down the winding road to Udine.

All we know of the war is that the Germans are in the castle. We of the brotherhood have a radio, and we follow the strange course of the war as if it were some extended game whose rules aren't clear, even to the players. But perhaps today we will learn more of it. Antonio, whose duty it is to listen to the radio, told me this morning that Marshall Badoglio has declared war on Germany. That means that the Germans, who were our friends, are now our enemies, and the mysterious people in the castle are now an occupying force. We are all encouraged to join the resistance, though so far there has been nothing to resist. We are told that the Germans are brutal, that they rape women and murder little children. Our women in their black shawls and black dresses with their rotten teeth are no great incitement to rape. They even tie handkerchiefs around their knees so that the sight of so much flesh will not unduly excite their husbands. Still, there are enough children around, though I sometimes wonder whether the joys of the flesh or the need for another hand in the fields is the chief inducement to lust in our village.

This year, I am in charge of the cattle. Each morning, I drive them high into the mountains to feed on the sparse grasses, and at night I return them to their shed, which, as in every other house in our village, is directly below our living quarters. I look forward to the snows, when the cattle will have to stay in, and I will only have to throw them their hay and milk them. Then, through the long dark winter days I will play chess with Mario or Emilio, or one of the others whose work will not take him from the house. Last year I was the fisher and could spend my time in the cool of the forest under the beeches, the larch and the towering Norwegian spruces. I was clever at that, and I caught more trout and eels than we seven could eat. Sometimes I would even catch a sturgeon, and though the old ones speak of a time when sturgeon were plentiful, they are rare enough now. Next year I will be the carpenter, and though my hands are not good with wood, it will be better than sitting on the side of this mountain in the dry, cold wind that never, even for a moment, lets up.

Sandro

Giorgio tells me that something is happening at the castle. From the pasture in the mountains he can see over the walls into the courtyard. There is now a large black limousine parked with the army trucks. Someone very important has come, though there is no gossip in the village. Whoever it is must have arrived at night with the convoy of trucks. He says he thinks he saw a woman in a white dress walk to the gate, then hurry back to the castle door, but he is a half mile away and it is unlikely he could have seen that. Herding the cattle is the worst job. There is nothing to do but sit, and sometimes the imagination takes over. When it was my turn, I too saw strange things.

I think I may have made a very bad mistake. One of the drivers stopped his jeep and asked me the way to the castle. Without thinking, I answered him in German. He seemed surprised, though he said nothing. It is difficult enough for a dwarf to escape notice without advertising his presence by speaking languages he should not speak. Gian Petro says that the time of our mission is near. I hope so. I have waited twenty years in this place, knowing only my own part of the mission and sworn not to tell or ask of the others' parts. On the day that Gian Petro gives the word that the mission must begin, then we shall all know. Now, even he knows only the signs that will release us to our acts.

Once again, the spring has failed. Gian Petro tells us that once this was the most fertile valley in all of Italy. In spring the vineyards on the slopes sprang into life and the air was so heavy with the fragrance of blossoms you were made dizzy by it. Then, he says, the cattle were fat and didn't have to be driven up into the mountains, because the grass was so lush that when they ate one blade, another leaped up to take its place.

Then, the air was heavy with bees, and a thousand different kinds of birds woke you with their singing every day. The peasants sang at their work, and there were festivals for every occasion, the Festival of the Spring Flowers, the Festival of the Jousting of the Queens, the Winemakers' Festival, the Festival of the Shoemakers' Guild and a hundred others.

Now, there are no festivals. The air itself seems to be poisoned. When the bora blows from the east, the leaves on trees shrivel and crack. When the clouds come in from the south, the rains wash away a whole summer's work. From the north come snows that bury us and untimely frost that kill the young buds. Only the west wind brings us hope, but the wind is almost never from the west.

I have tended the vines with immaculate care, tying them into hearts as my father taught me to do at home in the Moselle valley, but where there should be a riot of leaves there are now only a few sickly buds. At home the wine was amber and tasted like honey. Here, I will produce once more a wine that is pale and sour. Only the vegetables that hide underground can survive: turnips, potatoes, carrots and parsnips.

Perhaps the Germans know that, and that is why they are searching all the houses. Three more truckloads came in today. Large humourless men who surrounded all the houses in the village, then searched them from top to bottom. They found nothing, of course. The houses are all above ground. The few partisans we have are frightened young men who hide in the caves lower in the valley, and have no weapons to oppose the occupiers.

Antonio

Listen. Through the spit and crackle of the radio set you can hear all the voices of Babel: French, German, Italian, English, Russian, Spanish, Dutch, Arabic, so many languages, so many lies being told. After each battle, all sides proclaim themselves winners, so much destroyed, so many killed, bridges blown up, factories exploded. They taunt each other in each other's language, they urge the people at home to sacrifice for final victory, so many glorious countries, so much fighting to pre-serve civilization from the maddened hordes outside.

After a while, you know them all, all the languages. They say the same things in the same rhythms so that you learn that meaning is not in the words but in the patterns, some grammar common to them all for which the words are merely clothing. And somehow, somewhere in the gaps between what is said runs a thin line of truth, a delicate wavering line that breaks and rejoins, disappears into the welter of words, then re-appears. This is the line I listen to, this thin band of silence that carries the current of events.

I have listened for so long now that I hardly need my other senses. I make my way home down the steep mountain path from my cave by the sound of the water rippling in a distant stream, the whistle of wind over rocks, the nodding and rustling of trees. I hear the earth's exhalations, the moisture in the earth being drawn upwards by the sun. As I approach the town, I hear the women roll over in their beds, I hear the men scratch themselves. I can hear the scurry of mice in attics, the spinning of spiders' webs, the grass growing and leaves unfurling. If I stand very still, I can hear into the hearts of atoms, the electrons swirling around their nuclei.

And so I know this war is nearly over. Through the radio's static I can hear the tanks moving upward from the south. Rome fell today, and I could hear the sounds of rejoicing in the streets. It will still be a while before the troops get this far north, and so we must be very careful. We are like a patient with an evil growth in the heart. We must be careful that the operation that removes that growth does not kill us all. I have warned the partisans to keep to their caves. Events larger than them are shaping history, and it is better they be alive to farm when this is over, than some German car should be destroyed.

Someone is being held in the castle, someone who is more important than any single battle. Giorgio has seen her from the pasture above the castle, a woman in a white dress who is rarely allowed into the grounds. I believe I can hear her weeping as I circle the castle on my way home from the listening cave.

Von Ribbentrop himself has been to see her several times. He comes in the dead of the night and is gone again by morning. I thought perhaps she was his daughter, but I no longer think so. The radio from the castle reports in a code I cannot understand. It sounds like the random static you hear when there are sunspots.

Guido

They splish and they splash, these trout, they dance on their tails. When the weather is good, they are eager for the net. They say to each other, "Look, Guido is here again, we will tease him with our dancing, then, when he is frantic with worry that he will catch nothing, we will swim into his net." The eels, they are another thing, the eels, they are evil. They glide so silently over the shallow beds of streams, they hide in the deep holes, they are like the snake that tempted poor Eve when she was all innocence and could not have known better. They eat birds, yes they do, those eels, they eat baby ducklings. The mother has a brood of ten, then in one silent swallow so that she does not even know it has happened, she has a brood of nine.

But worst of all is the dark one, Old Snapper, who hides in the depths of the deepest pools. Sometimes, you think you see a log, just below the surface, something darker than the darkness of deep water, but when you see him, it is already too late, because he always sees you first and is gone. The others are all proud because they caught sturgeon, but they never caught Old Snapper, and what is the good of catching any other? I have caught them too, sturgeon I mean, but I have let them go. The trout are fine because they know they are food, and they like to be caught, and the eels are fine because they are evil and deserve to be eaten, but a sturgeon is no good unless he is Old Snapper, because every mouthful you eat reminds you that Old Snapper is still there, at the bottom of some pool, laughing at you.

It is going to be harder to catch him, now that winter has come and the snow is piled along the banks of the streams. In some places, there is ice, but the ice is treacherous. A German soldier fell through the ice, and if Old Snapper has not eaten him, he is at the bottom of a pool. In the spring he will rise and be tumbled down the stream until his clothing catches on to a root or a twig, and we will find him and take him to the priest to bury.

Old Snapper and the German soldier will have to wait until another day. Today I must catch trout. Since the girl of milk and blood has come to live with us, I must see that we have fresh trout every day. It was me who found her, little Guido who everyone pats on the head because I am happy and I sing. I took her from the woodcutter, who is a good man but full of fear. He found her wandering under the larches in her white robe with three drops of blood on her breast. Her eyes are the palest blue, and her long hair is so white that it looks silver. Her complexion is the colour of milk. The woodcutter says she escaped from the castle. She was terrified and didn't want to go back. The woodcutter didn't know what to do. If the people from the castle caught him with the girl, they would kill him, and so he brought her to us, to me, little Guido. I took her to a cave that only I know, and lit a fire. Then when it was dark, I went for the others, and we carried her home wrapped in a blanket. Gian Petro says it is the start of our mission. We must protect her until other things come clear. That night, I was given an extra portion of the evening rum, then I sang a song for them, a song about a little bird that is pierced by a thorn, but who sings so beautifully that all the animals of the forest weep, until their tears become a river and a golden boat floats down the river with a handsome prince who rescues the little bird, who is really a princess. When I was finished, the girl of milk and blood kissed me on the forehead, and since then I have been so filled with joy, my heart is ready to burst.

She is good, the girl of milk and blood, so good that thinking of her goodness can bring any of us to tears. Her skin is so delicate that anything that touches it leaves a bruise. She says she must do her part in our household, and so she mends our clothes. Last night, a needle pricked her thumb and splattered three drops of blood onto her white robe, so that she was just as I found her. She fainted, and when she awoke, she could remember nothing, only that she is terrified of the castle. Gian Petro says it is a warning of danger. He says we must go about our business as if nothing had happened, and he has cautioned the girl of milk and blood not to open the door to any knock. I think if I could catch Old Snapper, the dark one, everything would work out right. I have mentioned this to the others, but they tell me that is nonsense. Still, I think I know how it can be done, not with a net, but with a line, and a lure made from a piece of cloth with three drops of blood.

Rico

Today my hands shake, the chisel turns and twists, making gouges in the wood. Gian Petro says I can have no day of rest, but must continue making sabots. We are in terrible danger, he says, and so we must go on as if nothing had happened or else our mission will be lost. I think it is lost already with the loss of the girl. We should never have tried to live our ordinary lives. We should have taken her to the deepest cave and hidden her away until it was safe. We have supplies sufficient for a year, and if the war still raged, we might spirit her away to the south, to freedom.

Now the house is still with an awful silence. All that joy that bubbled through the house these last three months is gone. The walls seem still to hold the echo of her songs, and the ripple of her laugh hovers in the corner of the room. And still we have no idea who she was, no more idea than she had herself. She was like, not a new-born child, but a new-born woman. Her innocence was amazing, a purity so great that it was palpable. Her hands were so delicate she could never have done a stitch of work in her life. And yet she learned, she learned quickly. We would have done everything for her, but Gian Petro said, no, she was not a plaything. She would have to work for her keep like the rest of us.

And work she did. She darned our clothes and washed them cleaner than they had ever been. She swept the floor and made the beds and cooked our meals. At first, she had to be shown how to do the simplest things, how to thread a needle, how to hold a broom, how to start a fire. But once she had learned, she made us feel awkward and clumsy just watching her grace.

Her skin was so delicate that anything might bruise it, and she cut herself often. Then she would bleed, though never more than a few drops. Her cuts would heal miraculously in a day, but the bruises lasted for weeks, tingeing the whiteness of her skin with blue. She cooked the most wonderful meals, but would eat nothing herself except a little milk and, occasionally, to please Guido, a mouthful of trout. She was frightened of the eels and refused to touch them. When Gian Petro insisted she cook them, I took a few moments away from my chisels and cooked them for her. It was a small deception.

The plants in our house are starting to droop, mourning for her, though I water them every day. When she arrived, they burst into a profusion of leaves, as if it were already spring. She spoke to them, encouraged the tiny buds, called white flowers out of plants that had never flowered before, white flowers with a touch of scarlet at the centre.

I wept while I made the coffin, staining the glass with my tears. Giorgio wept in the cattle shed, and the cattle wept with him. Sandro and Mario wept over their game of chess, and Antonio says he could hear nothing over the radio but the sound of distant weeping. Only Gian Petro did not weep, but his eyes were tense and bewildered, full of fear in a way I have never seen before. He brought me the glass, from where I do not know, and he told me my craft would be tested as never before. In spite of my grief, I was proud when we laid her in the coffin of glass. Every detail was perfect, the glass cut and fitted and sealed so there was no sign of joining, no hint of workmanship, no evidence of the craft that was behind the art. The coffin was as perfect as any jewel, as impervious to the elements as any rock.

Someone is responsible, and I fear it may be me. We were warned never to leave her alone, even for a second, and she was warned never to open the door to any knock. I had gone to the cattle shed for a moment to speak with Giorgio. Sandro and Mario left their game of chess for a moment to bring her an icicle from the roof because she had teased them into getting it for her. She loved to suck on icicles like a child with a frozen treat. Antonio was at his listening post and Guido was fishing in his frozen stream. Gian Petro was in the village as usual. There was a knock, there must have been a knock, she opened the door, she must have opened it herself against all the warnings, and when I returned she was dead, a piece of apple lodged in her throat. The rest of the apple sat on the table, its skin as red as blood, its flesh as white as milk.

Gian Petro was in a rage when he returned a few moments later. I could tell him nothing, only confess my lack of responsibility, my failure. Sandro and Mario, from their position on the roof, saw a flapping of black rags in the street, like a giant crow, but thought it was only one of the crones of the village passing. A sudden cold wind nearly blew them from the roof, and they had to cling to the chimney until it passed.

Then, that terrible night, the coldest night of the year, we carried her in her coffin up into the mountain. Gian Petro broke the trail through the deep snow, and we six struggled behind him, stumbling on our tiny legs, though the coffin with its treasure inside weighed no more than a tiny bird. It was both the lightest and the heaviest load I have ever had to bear.

And now what are we to do? There is no longer any point to the making of sabots or the catching of eels, no point to the raising of cattle or the making of wine, no point to the working of metal or to listening to the reports of a war about which I no longer care. My heart tells me that this war will never end, that spring will never come again. We shall only have war and winter, winter and war.

Mario

This place is full of fear and pain. In the darkness of this dungeon we replay a medieval battle of light against darkness, good against evil. Throughout history, this castle has been the head of the valley, the centre from which wisdom and morality spread to the sprawling body of the community, but now there is a cancer working here, a foreign body that has seized control and whose evil seeps outward, infecting the whole.

The villagers led the Nazis to our door, and who can blame them, full of fear and superstition, trying to save themselves at any cost. They have allied themselves with a failing demon, though they cannot know that. They clustered around the soldiers who dragged us from our beds, they jeered and shouted and their faces were filled with hate, our weakness as hateful to them as the Nazis' strength.

The war will be over in a few days, but that will be too late for us. We are in the coils of a dying but still-dangerous monster. At dawn the firing squad, they have told us, after our week of pain. And so our mission fails, or else we have done our part in some larger plan that has no further use for us. The girl was innocence itself, she loved and mothered us, and her death, I think, is the death of innocence and goodness in this world. Perhaps the Nazis will be replaced with some even larger evil, though it is hard to think what evil might be greater.

We have been tortured and mutilated beyond anything I thought the human body could bear. And they used the tools of my trade, the metalworker's tools, pincers and tongs and fire. They have slowly removed our fingernails, crushed our arms and legs, set fire to our hair and carved their hateful symbol in our flesh with a burning poker. We have told them nothing, though there is nothing to tell but the location of a mountain grave, a glass coffin and a body they might defile but could not offer pain. Tomorrow they will ask us one more time, then they will pour the hot lead of bullets into our bodies, whatever our answer.

I am almost eager for that death. See us for what we were, what we are. Our bodies stunted and deformed, half men always on the lookout for the kick, the beating that the others must give because we affront them by wrapping desire in such awkward flesh. We are comic at a distance, terrifying when we're near, conjuring in every man the dwarf within.

And though I am eager, I am sick with loss. I yearn for one more taste of the water from a cool stream, for the scent of roses on a heavy summer day, for the scratch of wool on my skin. I want to see clouds low over the mountains, to hear Guido sing a song full of joy. I ache for the world that will end in the morning.

Here in this tiny dark cell we seven are huddled as if we were one flesh. We cannot tell whose moan we hear, even when it is our own. The warm blood we feel is ours communally, the fear we share, one common fear. Only Gian Petro has hope and his soft voice is murmuring words of comfort, but it is too late. Hope is the final torture, the last delusion. We have given our lives to a mission that is probably a failure, may even have been a chimera from the start.

Now, the first rays of dawn will be spreading from the east. The soldiers will be oiling their guns and preparing the blindfolds. There will be one large grave waiting in the courtyard, a bag of quicklime beside it. They will be so intent on their task that perhaps they will not hear the soft thunder of the bombs that rock even our cell below the castle, the distant rumbling of the guns.

Gian Petro

This is a spring that takes itself seriously, that believes in the history of transformations and is not satisfied with the simple mechanics of budding and flowering. When the bomb landed on the castle, opening the cocoon of our cell, I stepped across the broken bricks of the wall into a blazing dawn. The clouds had curled themselves into balls of cumulus and were dreaming along the horizon to the south. I looked for the others, Giorgio, Sandro, Antonio, Guido, Rico, Mario, but they had disappeared. I reached my long arms into the air, stretched my long legs, felt the strength ripple through my body. Then I heard the voices inside me. Little Guido, whispering to me, told me where to look for Old Snapper, the dark one. Giorgio told me where the cattle liked to feed, Rico sent a message to my fingers telling me the exact pressure of a chisel on wood, Mario sent a vision of a bracelet wound from gold chains, and Antonio let me hear the whistle of crickets in a distant stream.

And then I knew that the first miracle had occurred. In the crucible of that exploding bomb, our mass of deformed dwarf-flesh had separated into atoms, then reformed into molecules. The molecules had re-knit themselves into amino acids and proteins, shaped themselves into complex chains, twisted and curled into the only possible body. The accidental electricity of that explosion had charged that body with life and filled each neuron and synapse of the brain with seven memories. It had concentrated all the ghosts of the castle, all thoughts that had been thought there, all the passions that had seeped into the stone walls of the castle and delivered them to us, to me. I realized that I had been born that second, and so I named myself. Gian Petro.

When Gian Petro stepped into the courtyard, out of the ruins of the castle, he saw that thousands of mushrooms had sprung up during the night. They formed a soft bed, like velvet, and as he strode across them, crushing them, they exuded a delicate milky substance that smelled, not unpleasantly, like bleach. Beyond the gates of the castle, the open field that led to the village was filled with snow-white flowers, each with a core of crimson. Along the wall that separated field from road, the vines were covered with mauve trumpet flowers that whispered to him softly. There were bees everywhere, humming ecstatically.

The village was full of music. People were singing and dancing in the streets. An old man played a violin, dancing as he played, and a young man accompanied him on an accordion. The villagers had shed their winter black and were dressed in bright reds and yellows and blues. A pretty girl swirled by, her red dress so bright it seemed in flames. Her lover wore a white shirt, open at the neck, with a brilliant red bandanna. "Baron," they called to Gian Petro, "the war is over. The war is over." He smiled at his people's joy, but he kept walking through the village, past the tables heaped with food and wine, past the donkeys with garlands around their necks, down the winding path into the valley.

The grass was so lush along the pathway that sometimes it was hard to tell where it wound. The vineyards along the slope were a riot of leaves, and the grapes, though not yet ripe, seemed ready to burst with sweetness. Underground, the roots were burying themselves deep, searching for water. They passed underground messages up through the sap to the highest leaves of the trees. Brilliant birds flashed yellow and red in the blur of green.

The baron continued onward, down through the valley into the forest. Under the pine and spruce, it was cool, and sunlight dappled the carpet of needles. He came to a small, fast-running stream and followed it to a pool deep in the heart of the forest. There, the body of the drowned soldier had surfaced. It was surrounded by a mass of white water lilies, and water lilies seemed to be growing out of the flesh. Gian Petro pulled the body from the pool and laid it gently on the grassy shore. Then he drew a line and hook from his pocket and baited the hook with the white root of a small willow. He tossed out his line into the pool, and the dark one rose to the bait. Gian Petro pulled him in without effort and laid him on the bank beside the dead soldier. They were exactly the same size, and from a small distance, it was impossible to tell them apart.

Gian Petro followed the stream a little further, until it turned, then he continued up the mountain on the other side of the valley. The trees soon became sparser and were replaced with gentian and saxifrage and rock jasmine. When he reached the very top of the mountain where the glass coffin lay, he saw that it was surrounded by snowdrops and tiny red blood-flowers. He strode across the carpet of flowers, not caring how the sap bled from the tiny plants he crushed. He opened the lid of the glass coffin, picked up the girl and laid her down in the flowers. The piece of apple that had stuck in her throat came free, and she breathed. Her pale white cheeks turned red with life as he took her in his arms. He spoke to her of love in his seven voices, and as they loved, the discreet sun hid his face behind a cloud. Every living thing reached up eagerly to the gentle rain that followed.